Series Note: Although set in the same futuristic world, all of the stories in the Interstellar Service & Discipline series may be read as standalone books. Lost Star is the prequel to Victorious Star.

Once upon a time, before the Victorious Star, there were a prince and a prisoner . . .

Aubrey was a tech engineer with a dirty little secret that the Moribund Company was willing to destroy everyone and everything to get their hands on. When Deshryt Seht, blood prince of Skeldhor, saved the dying boy's life, it set off a contest of wills as strong as the call of their blood.

Unfortunately, Aubrey has one more secret that severs their relationship before it can truly begin.

Though years and an ocean of stars separate the prince from the prisoner he saved, neither the prince nor the Moribund Company will let him escape. What was Lost will be found, winner take all.

Publisher's Note: This book contains explicit sexual content, graphic language, and situations that some readers may find objectionable: Anal play/intercourse, substantial BDSM elements (including/not limited to bondage, domination/submission, whipping), menage (m/m/f), and homoerotic sexual situations (m/m, f/f).

Lost Star
Copyright © 2019 Morgan Hawke
ISBN: 978-1-4874-2634-7
Cover art by Martine Jardin

Published by eXtasy Books Inc or
Devine Destinies, an imprint of eXtasy Books Inc

Look for us online at:
www.eXtasybooks.com or www.devinedestinies.com

Lost Star
Interstellar Service and Discipline Book 4
Prequel to: Victorious Star

By

Morgan Hawke

CHAPTER ONE

"Look, you rusting pile of antique junk! I'm trying to save your ass here! Let me in!" Aubrey grabbed his throat, gasping for breath, and choked. The air on the freighter's sub-engineering deck was thick and foul with smoke from melted metal and fused wiring. "Morris! Are you listening to me?" He slammed his bruised fist against the control console, nearly knocking over the small light he'd rigged. Most of the lights had gone out in the first hit from the marauders. He didn't want to think about how close they had come to losing all life support, too.

"I hear you, tech engineer." The ship's tired and masculine mind-voice shimmered with a touch of annoyance across the wire jacked into the back of Aubrey's skull. "You do not have clearance for access. You are not the nav-pilot."

Aubrey fought to calm his beating heart, not that his heart was listening. "Morris, your nav-pilot is dead. He's dead with everyone else that was on your bridge. If you don't let me in, we'll be boarded, and you'll be torn apart for scrap!"

"I am already . . . scrap." Crushing depression and electronic interference colored the electronic mind-voice.

"I know you're old. Fate, damn you! But you're not dead yet!" Aubrey scrubbed a hand through what little hair he had left, nearly dislodging the jack in the back of his skull. Damned military-issue buzz-cut freaking itched. He leaned over the panel. "Morris, please! Let me in! There isn't anybody else with an array to talk to you and I'm not fucking ready to die yet!" His breath hitched. Fate, he hadn't even

1

reached the legal age to drink yet. He closed his stinging eyes and took a deep breath. "And neither are the rest of the men on this ship. If you want to die, then fine, die! But let me save the ones who want to live first!"

Anger flickered deep in the ship's sentience.

Aubrey held his breath. Apparently, his comment about letting the crew die had pissed the ship off. That was good, very good. There was still a chance. If he could get access to the ship's controls, he could use the freighter's fully functional pulse cannons to clear a hole and try for a jump. If the ship didn't kill him with a power burst instead.

Information slammed into his skull to become sight, sound, taste, smell . . . and pain, hideous wrenching pain. Aubrey gasped and dropped to his knees. The ship was in agony. There were gaping holes all over the ship's hull. Wounds that bled air, water, and bodies . . . Bodies of people he knew.

Sheer stubborn will and deep terror forced him back up on his feet. He ignored the itch of tears streaking down his smoke-smeared face and threw every code he had into the ship's controls, grabbing for everything that still worked.

He found everybody still breathing and began opening doors, making safe passages for the crew to get deeper into the ship where he could do something about maintaining life support.

At the same time, he activated the pulse cannons and aimed them at the corsair closing in to make contact against the starboard side. He knew that at this close range, he was going to damage the freighter more, but he could not afford to let the marauders board. They were only a small freighter with no military personnel capable of defending them, none still alive anyway. Once they got in, the game was over. They were utterly defenseless.

Aubrey smiled grimly and opened fire.

The pulse cannons burned a surgically precise hole right

through the attacking ship's engineering core. The ship's sensors delivered a low casualty rating from the other ship, but all maneuver controls were offline.

The attacking ship veered off course diving right under them.

Aubrey shouted in triumph. "That's right, you stupid-assed shit-heels! The body manning these cannons actually knows what to fucking hit!" Abruptly, he lost clear sight of the second corsair. The ship's sensors were going out on the keel. They were in deep trouble if he didn't get them back in view.

Information trickled in from the remaining corsair. It was a sentience to sentience communication. It was meant to be hidden from the nav-pilot.

Aubrey smiled grimly. If he'd had a piloting array, he would have missed it, but he didn't. He had a programming array. His ability to interpret the ship's complete interior and exterior data was somewhat limited, nothing compared to the near physical connection a nav-pilot had. On the other hand, what he did have was one of the most complete mind to mind connections one could get with a ship.

And he'd been a very bad boy before the Agency had caught up with him.

He intercepted the communication without even trying. At the same time, he worked feverishly to reroute power to the sensors so he could see well enough to get a nice clean shot on the corsair dangerously close to his keel.

His personally doctored programs read the encrypted communications with pathetic ease. Those same programs were the reason he had been arrested and penal chipped, but they continued to prove useful every now and again.

The only reason the Agency hadn't fried his ass when they finally caught him, was because he'd been under-age, a minor, with no fatalities to his name. Instead, the Agency had offered him the chance to work off his sentence using his programming tech talents on whatever ship they posted him to.

It was that or a memory wipe.

He'd been grateful for the chance to keep all his hard-won codes and skills, and it had gotten him off-planet. As far as he was concerned, getting off that industrial waste of a planet had been worth being penal chipped.

The past two and a half Imperial standard years of being passed from ship to ship as a programming tech engineer hadn't been all that hard. The food sucked, but the work was simplistic compared to the programming stuff he'd done for sheer entertainment. The bulk of it was system updates. His mouth occasionally got him into trouble, but his rating as a minor had saved his ass from more than one disciplinary reaming. He smiled sourly. Thank the Fates for a scrawny graceless build that made him look years younger than he actually was.

He only had six more months to the end of his sentence — and his legal majority. Once he was free of the penal chip in the back of his skull, he had a nice long well-paying career ahead of him. He planned to get thoroughly drunk and thoroughly laid to celebrate his new life as a free man. If he lived that long. He sighed and focused on the coded communications being relayed.

The corsair was inquiring about damages.

Morris offered his external damage report and the fact that his nav-pilot was dead, without mentioning that they were still jump capable.

Aubrey grinned. Apparently, Morris wasn't ready to give up yet.

'Surrender. Will relocate sentience.'

He nodded. The other ship was trying to make some kind of a deal. That was pretty much expected. Obviously, they were after the ship's experienced sentience. There wasn't a damned thing on this old freighter that would interest marauders. They weren't carrying weapons.

'No survivors.'

No survivors? Aubrey sucked in a breath. But there were some seventy-odd people still breathing on this ship? He shot a line of data toward the other ship describing his survivors.

'Cut life support.'

What? Aubrey frowned. That had to have been a misinterpretation of the coded transmission. He inserted a message into the encrypted communication. *Please repeat last transmission.*

'No survivors. Disengage all life support.'

Aubrey gasped. *Son of a fucking bitch!* They wanted Morris to kill every living person on this ship? He ground his teeth. *Fuck that shit!* Out of sheer temper, he slammed a hijack code he'd made to catch small yachts for joyrides into the ship's connecting data stream. To get it past the preliminary firewalls, he added a doctored breaker-code and aimed the whole mess straight for their engineering console, bypassing their nav-pilot.

He'd been a very, *very* bad boy before the Agency nailed him.

Aubrey figured that the breaker-code wouldn't make it very far. The other craft was a corsair and far more sophisticated than the yachts the code was designed for, but he figured he'd at least cause enough trouble to make a limping escape.

The other ship's data poured into his skull. Suddenly his vision of Morris and both corsairs was crystal clear. Aubrey gasped. *Holy shit!* He'd actually made connection.

A stream of bitching howled across the data stream.

Aubrey choked out a laugh. There was a very pissed off nav-pilot at the far end who had somehow found himself locked out of his own ship. Aubrey licked his dry lips and grabbed for control, telling the other ship to turn its ass around and make for jump. It was the only thing he could think of.

The ship fought his control. He wasn't giving it the right directives.

Grim humor colored Morris's sentience. "Like this boy . . ." Data streamed toward the other ship, bolstering Aubrey's commands.

The other ship turned away and their jump engines came online.

It was working? Aubrey rubbed sweat from his brow with his arm and checked his connection. It was solid. The other ship *was* taking his orders. Fate be damned, it was working! He threw back his head and shouted. "Take that you rat-bastards!" He hooted and punched the air, nearly knocking the cord from his skull jack. If there had been room to jump up and down, he would have done it.

Energy pulsed as folds of space unraveled and a third corsair wavered into local space nearly on their nose.

Every sensor on the ship burned white-hot, scoured by the energy backwash as space snapped back into place around the corsair catching Morris in the rebound.

Morris screamed in sensory overload.

Aubrey screamed with him. His array slammed all channels closed to protect the biological mind attached to it. The world receded to a pinprick of light at the very far end of a long black tunnel. He didn't even feel his chin smack hard on the engineering panel or his cheek hit the crash-littered deck plates.

CHAPTER TWO

Aubrey gasped awake strapped on his back to a table with the smell of antiseptic in his nose. He groaned. His entire body was one big mass of hurt. He tried to open his eyes and realized that they were already open. He'd been blinded. Someone had gotten into his internal array and turned off his eyes.

"Good morning, tech engineer." The voice was masculine, richly cultured, cool and amused.

Aubrey blinked, but the blackness remained. "Where am I?"

"You are on my ship. I am Moribund. I'm sure you will prove a very valuable addition to my company."

"Huh?" Aubrey jerked. He couldn't move an inch. "I can't be in your company. I'm penal indentured." He scowled. He was a convict, a legal slave until he finished off his sentence. The tattoo marking the data-chip in the back of his neck said so. "You have to go through the Agency penal board . . ."

"The chip has already been removed."

Aubrey froze. No way . . . They exploded when tampered with. "Then how come I'm not dead?"

"Because I have very talented staff." Moribund chuckled right next to his ear. "Of which you may count yourself a member."

Aubrey flinched back and every hair on his body rose. There was something very wrong with this man. He had no clue what, but he'd learned long ago to listen to those small hairs.

Moribund's boot heels thumped as he walked around Aubrey's feet to the other side of the table. Fabric rustled right next to Aubrey's left elbow. "Shall we discuss the terms of your service?"

Aubrey sighed and relaxed on the table. There wasn't a whole lot else he could do. "Sure. What do you want from me?"

"I want you to steal ships, the same way you took mine."

Aubrey's blood turned to ice. He was in the enemy's hands. He'd known he couldn't be anywhere else, but . . . But the last transmission he'd intercepted had said 'no survivors.' Aubrey turned his sightless eyes toward Moribund. "How many survivors from my ship?"

Moribund drew in a slow breath and released it. "You."

Aubrey struggled to interpret that another way and failed miserably. Him. He was the only survivor. His chest clenched and he drew in a shuddering breath. "You killed them."

"Your ship did."

Aubrey closed his eyes to keep in the fierce ache that threatened to spill. "Damn it, Morris . . ." He failed. Tears leaked from his eyes.

"I'm afraid that the ship's sentience did not survive the act. My nav-pilot tells me that it was deliberate."

Aubrey stilled. Morris had committed suicide? Then the ship had remained true . . . but, everyone that had been on him was still dead. He gasped for breath and shuddered with the sobs he refused to release. All of them . . . gone forever, except him.

"Some ships are that way. You make a capture only to lose the ship in the process. Very wasteful." Moribund paced at Aubrey's side. "The best way would be to erase the crews without the ship having to do it. This way I can keep the ship-mind intact." Moribund leaned close to Aubrey. "And that's why I want you. Somehow, you succeeded in usurping not only the nav-pilot but the sentience as well, taking complete control of my ship. With your talents, I could keep the ships I capture."

Aubrey jerked at whatever held him to the table. "I am not killing people for you!"

"How old are you, boy?"

Aubrey stilled. "Why?"

"My medic says you're below legal age."

Aubrey clenched his jaw. "So?"

"So?" Moribund's voice dropped to a whisper. "You cannot legally walk into a bar or a brothel. I doubt you've even had sex yet. Are you sure you want to die before you've even lived?"

Aubrey drew in a deep breath. "I will not kill people."

"Are you quite sure?"

Aubrey turned to face Moribund with blind eyes. "Fuck you." His voice vibrated with the hate that burned in his heart. "Go ahead and kill me. I belong with my murdered ship and crewmates."

"Very well then." He stepped back.

Aubrey was unbuckled and dragged from the table. He hit the deck hard and groaned. Painfully tight hands jerked him up onto his knees. His wrists were pulled behind his back and cuffed. They lifted him onto his feet and practically dragged him out of medical. After a fast walk down a long hall, he was jerked to a halt.

The mechanical sound of an airlock door opening crashed in his ears. He nearly dropped to his knees in shock. They really were going to kill him.

He was brutally shoved sideways and fell onto a very cold floor. The bare skin of his hands tried to stick to the metal. He fisted his hands and came up on his knees, listening as the airlock door closed.

The air hissed, thinned and chilled to razor sharpness with

incredible speed. He sucked in one last breath and tried not to scream. He didn't succeed.

Aubrey awoke curled on his side shaking on a bare, but warm deck. His mouth was full of thick copper-flavored liquid. Blood.

A booted foot pushed him onto his back and his cuffed hands. "Alas for your suicidal wishes, I am not inclined to let you die." Moribund's voice was politely regretful, but the humor behind it was blatantly obvious. "But you may visit the airlock again if you wish?"

Aubrey couldn't draw a full breath. His lungs were too full of liquid. He suspected that they were bleeding. He had to whisper. "Fine, put me back in, asshole."

They did.

Determined to kill himself outright, Aubrey tried to suck in the blade cold air and screamed it right back out.

He woke up on the deck, again. He coughed, spewing hot wet liquid that tasted strongly of copper, and other things. He winced. *Lung damage.* He wasn't dead, but he would be soon.

"There are faster ways to gain compliance. Pity I need your mind intact."

"Fuck . . . you." Aubrey barely got the words out.

Another trip to the airlock.

This time, he couldn't scream, his lungs were too full of ice for breath.

Aubrey awoke blind and floating in the warm heavy liquid of what could only be a medical tank. He'd been in one once before after a nasty glider spill. The thick liquid labored in, and then out, of his lungs. He couldn't move and his mind didn't want to process properly. He could barely think. He was still alive. Damnit.

Sleep crushed him under. He didn't fight it. Awareness was something he was not interested in having.

He dreamed, of sweeping starscapes and a gentle female presence. "Stay with me," she whispered. "Don't leave me. I don't want to be alone."

Out of sheer reflex, he reached out. He didn't want to be alone either.

She folded around him with lithe grace and warmth.

His body responded to her warmth. He reached for more, knowing it was a dream and wanting it to be more. He reached until he could almost feel softness under his hands and against his skin. The dream shifted, becoming a body intimately entwined with his. He could almost taste her mouth against his. His cock hardened.

She responded with shuddering delight and opened, offering herself.

He held her tight and arched into her. The impression of tight wet warmth blazed hot down his spine and concentrated around his cock. He clutched her to him, relishing the feeling of physical delight with another, something he had yet to have.

She moved against him, delivering the most riveting and delightful sensation he'd ever felt.

The sensation was so strong, he could feel his sleeping body bucking in response. He moved against her begging for more.

She complied with enthusiasm and reached for him. Abruptly, part of her entered him.

Delight speared through him and urgency tightened within him. Somewhere in the back of his mind an alarm went off, but the pleasure of her touch was so intense he didn't care. She was going to make him cum.

She touched him deeper.

Delight crested and release took him violently. The feeling of his balls emptying in something warm burned up his spine. His howl of release was muffled by the liquid in his lungs.

Then she took him again.

And again.

Aubrey awoke, still in the liquid tank, and still blind, but he wasn't alone. Someone was in his head with him. "Hello?"

"Hello, Aubrey." It was the female presence that had been in his dreams. "I am Niobe."

Awake and aware, Aubrey suddenly recognized the presence for what it was. He reeled in shock. It was the ship. He had made love to the ship. And it had been incredible.

A second presence, dark and sharp-edged, pressed against the edges of his mind.

Aubrey flinched back, but the presence remained on the edges of his mind. "What is that?"

"Don't look there." Niobe radiated sharp fear. "It's the nav-pilot. She will hurt you if she finds you looking."

"What?" He writhed away but couldn't gain any distance. "What is the nav-pilot doing in my head?" He shook his head in the tank and felt the pull of a data-jack plugged into the back of his head. Fuck. They had jacked into his mind and somehow gotten in past his firewalls and alarms. Anger burned. The firewalls weren't his only defense. He had other ways of dealing with intruders.

"No, you can't fight her."

"Oh yes, I can . . . ."

"No, you can't. You've been mapped. If you try to fight her, she will use your own programs against you."

"Mapped? I don't remember . . ."

"Yes, while you slept. You seemed to find the experience pleasurable."

"Pleasurable . . ." He flinched in shock. *The dream . . .* His mind had been mapped by a wet dream, giving Moribund access to his programs.

"Yes."

Anger burned in him. "Anything else I should know about?"

"You've been slave-drived and configured as an executable."

"What?" He sucked in a hard breath and his lungs labored with the additional liquid. "I'm an executable program? I'm something to turn on and shut down when you feel like it?"

She pulled back from him. "To the nav-pilot you are."

"No! I'm not a fucking program!" Something shifted in the back of his mind. He scanned the data being accessed; the hijack code and the breaker-code. Bleeding Fate . . ."Niobe, are we attacking a ship?"

"Yes."

"No. I won't kill people!"

"Aubrey, you are not killing anyone, the nav-pilot is."

"It's my program . . . .!"

"You're not executing it, the nav-pilot is."

"It's still my program and it's being used to kill people!" Aubrey gathered himself for a hard shove. "I will not do this!"

"No, don't! You don't want to touch her mind!"

"Why the hell not?"

"Aubrey, she's insane, she could kill you."

Aubrey grabbed for the stream of data. "Then I die. I'm supposed to be dead anyway."

The stream was pried out of his hold.

No! He used every trick he had to stop the data flow . . . and couldn't. He tried to erase the code. It was one of his favorites and he hated the idea of killing it, but he would not let his code be used in this way . . . and couldn't. Despite the fact that his programs were in his own encoding language, somehow a passcode had tacked on, sealing it off. He didn't have access to his own data.

"No! I won't do this!" Aubrey fought the restraints that held him, jerking hard and twisting to dislodge the jack in his head. Something rushed into his veins, numbing his brain and slowing his thoughts. Sleep began to press hard against his mind. He was being drugged.

"Yes," Niobe whispered. "You're being given a sedative."

"It's to keep me from fighting them."

"You cannot fight them. It's to keep you from hurting yourself."

The data stream stopped. They had gained access. Somewhere out there, a ship was killing her crew. And it was his fault. Thick black guilt squeezed his heart even as his body stilled in response to the drugs in his blood. "Niobe, if I can't keep them out, I need to die. I won't be used to kill people."

"You will not die."

Aubrey fought to hold onto consciousness. "Niobe, I can't live this way, as a program to be used."

"You will live."

"I can't . . ."

"You will."

Sleep crushed him under.

Aubrey awoke, still blind, still in the tank, with someone rummaging around in his head. He slammed doors closed, only to have them pried open. He changed passcodes and re-arranged his files only to have them changed on him. He pulled every firewall and blocking trick he could think of . . . and they still got in.

He howled in fury and slammed a thick wall of anger at whoever was digging in his head.

A fist of moldering acidic rot closed around his mind. "Bad boy," it hissed. "Give me . . ." Barbed burning things squirmed through his wall of anger and burrowed deep into his mind, eating their way into his thoughts.

He screamed and shoved away from it. "Get out! Get out of my head!"

It didn't let him go. "Give me now!"

"No!" He writhed in an acid bath that tore his thoughts to shreds and ate the pieces. He thrashed in the tank and tried to scream.

Hands grasped the acid things and pulled them away. "Nav-pilot stop!" Niobe's mental voice vibrated with anger and terror. "You're causing damage!"

Aubrey gasped in shuddering relief. The liquid in the tank hid his tears.

"Bad boy! Give me what I want!"

"Nav-pilot not this way!" Niobe moved between them, pushing the acidic touch from his mind. "Give me access, and I'll get it for you."

"How?"

Comfort spilled across Aubrey's mind. Erotic pleasure spilled down his spine and poured into his cock. He froze in shock. "Niobe? What are you doing?" Her presence filled his mind and molded around him with the powerful sensation of flesh against flesh. His body responded. He couldn't stop it. "Niobe!"

"Oh," the nav-pilot purred. "Seduction."

Sensation raced through his body. Phantom kisses and caresses that he could feel but weren't there. He fought the drugging pull of rising climax, but his body wanted the pleasure of release she was offering. "Niobe, please! Don't do this to me." His balls tightened with urgency. He was going to cum, and when he did, she would take whatever it was the nav-pilot was after. "Niobe! This is rape."

"I know." Her mental voice echoed with regret and entered him.

He came, bucking hard. His mind opened under the

whitewash of blinding pleasure.

She speared deeper into him, burning him with searing delight.

He shuddered and felt climax rise again. "Niobe don't!" He fought his body's animal reactions and couldn't. "Niobe please!"

"I'm sorry, Aubrey, but they will have your compliance, or they will kill you. I will not let you die."

He came again, screaming into the liquid.

Time passed marked by dreams of swimming through an ocean of stars punctuated by stronger dreams of sex. Aubrey fought against the visceral pleasure pouring into his body, knowing that his mind was being taken while he cried out in release.

Niobe's sweet nature made it difficult to fight her. She had to be the gentlest ship-mind he'd ever had contact with. Her affection and desperate sorrow throbbed against his mind every time she brought him to unwilling release, but her conviction that she was saving him from certain death made her continue.

He pleaded with her to let him go, to let him die.

She wouldn't. He was the only thing she had, and she would not let him go. She pleaded with him to forget them, to just let go and let them take what they wanted.

He would not stop fighting. What they were using him for was wrong.

She knew and regretted it deeply. He could feel how she ached with every death her ship caused. But she took him anyway.

CHAPTER THREE

Aubrey awoke feeling the liquid bubbling around him. They were draining the tank. His head cleared the liquid, but his eyes still refused to function. He could hear voices, but his ears were too full of liquid to make out what they were saying. He sucked in a breath to ask what was going on.

His body revolted and he spewed viscous liquid from his mouth and nose. His head, lungs, and stomach ached long before he was done. The air was ice cold compared to the warm bath of the tank.

He was released from the harness and pulled from the tank naked. Aubrey counted four hands, so two people. He collapsed into their hands, too weak to lift his head.

He was lifted onto an antigrav table and floated somewhere. Moments later, the table stopped, and hot water sprayed down on him.

He jerked in alarm.

Hands held him down on the table. They washed every inch of him in the most impersonal manner possible. After a humiliating eternity, the bath finally ended, and Aubrey was helped upright and then onto his feet.

He wavered off balance between them. His ears abruptly cleared.

"There that wasn't so bad." The voice was deep, an older male.

"At least this one isn't augmented to hell and gone." The second voice seemed even older and also male.

"According to medical, he's not augmented at all. If he was

augmented, we could have used force cuffs to hold him upright."

Aubrey smiled sourly. "Sorry to disappoint you." It felt strange to use his mouth to talk.

The first man snorted. "Oh, so your ears are working after all?"

"Yeah." He shivered. "But my eyes are all messed up."

"Tank liquid." Fingers dug into his left upper arm to keep him balanced on his feet and turned Aubrey to the side. "You look wasted, but your muscles appear to be working just fine."

Aubrey rolled his eyes. "My muscles are not working fine. I can barely stand."

One of the men snorted. "You've been getting some kind of exercise in there, or you wouldn't be able to stand at all."

Aubrey frowned. All those dreams of swimming through stars . . . Had he been exercised while he slept?

The water collector went on with a loud howl, sucking all the moisture from the air in seconds.

Aubrey shivered. It was cold in the room. He was shoved forward between them. The tile under his bare feet became metal plate and he was stopped.

Hands cupped his elbows. "Lift your foot."

Aubrey lifted his foot and was helped into what felt like a full-body ship-suit. The fabric was thickly padded, warm and very welcome. He sealed it closed with fumbling fingers. "How long?"

Socks were tugged onto his feet. "How long what, kid?"

"How long have I been in the tank?" Aubrey lifted his feet for a pair of boots.

"Um, let's see . . ."

The boots were fastened closed. The damned things actually fit better than his last pair he'd worn. Aubrey felt something itching on his neck. He scratched at it and discovered that it was his own hair. It was past his shoulders. He froze. He'd been in the tank long enough for his hair to grow that long from a buzz-cut?

"I'm not sure. You've been in that tank since I got onboard three cycles ago."

Aubrey lifted his head. "*Three* thirty-day cycles?"

"Oh, longer than that." The other man chuckled. "I'm thinking at least two more."

Aubrey felt his knees shake beneath him. "*Five* cycles?" He was tugged forward and out into a carpeted hallway.

"Let's see, I think the limit is nine cycles and they told us to pull you because you'd reached limit."

Aubrey tripped on the carpet. "Are you saying I've been in that tank for nine cycles?" He couldn't grasp being in the tank that long. It hadn't seemed that long at all. "So now where am I going?"

"Right now? Where they told us to put you."

Aubrey dug in his heels. "You're not putting me in that tank again!"

The older man laughed. "Oh, hell no, you can't go back in there. Stay in there too long and you won't be able to function outside it." They tugged him forward.

Aubrey walked. It was that or be dragged. "Then what?"

"What were you in it for?"

Aubrey stiffened. They didn't know? "I was in it, I think, for lung damage."

"Lung damage?"

"That must have been some damage to need breathing liquid."

Aubrey clenched his jaw. "I suppose one too many visits to the airlock would do that."

"The airlock? Who'd you kill?"

"Who did *I* kill?" Aubrey chuckled and the chuckle became outright laughter. He threw back his head, laughing as the tears burned down his cheeks. He finally stopped, gasping for breath. "How many ships in the past nine months?"

"Are you okay, kid?"

Aubrey looked up with his sightless eyes and screamed. "How many ships did this fucking ship take in the past nine months?"

"Uh, forty-seven I think."

Aubrey's knees gave out and he dropped to his hands and knees. "Bleeding Fate . . ." There were hundreds of lives on some of those ships and thousands on others.

"Come on get up." They worked to pull him upright.

Aubrey climbed unsteadily onto his feet. "You want to know who I killed?" The hurt was so large he couldn't quite feel it. "I killed every bloody man aboard every bloody ship you took."

"What?"

"The kid's hysterical . . ."

Aubrey allowed them to tug him forward. He'd killed forty-seven ships. And he was going to kill more if they jacked him back into the ship. He couldn't physically fight them. He was completely blind and without a drop of physical augmentation. He couldn't mentally fight them — the ship was too strong and the nav-pilot was too crazy.

He had to die. It was the only way to stop the killing.

A vibration raced under Aubrey's feet. There was a distant howl of metal.

"What the hell was that?"

Aubrey smiled. He knew exactly what that was. He remembered it from his own ship. "We're under attack."

The man on Aubrey's right jerked. "We can't be . . ."

The man on his left released Aubrey's arm. "Yes, we can, I heard that we've been in Skeldhi space for two days now."

Aubrey blinked his blind eyes. Skeldhi space? That species had a particular hate for humans. A smile stretched his mouth. He didn't have one drop of code to get into their craft. He didn't have their coding language. He wouldn't be killing any ships today.

"What in bleeding fury are we doing in Skeldhi space?"

Aubrey released a chuckle. "Getting your asses blown away I'd say."

"Who the hell gave clearance to pull that kid from his tank?" The voice bellowed right in front of them.

Both men at Aubrey's elbows released him.

"Captain! Uh, it came from medical, sir!"

Aubrey frowned. That captain sounded nothing like Moribund.

"Yes, sir, Captain, sir! We got notification to pull him, clean him, get him dressed then take him to . . ." There was a pause. "Dock port seventy-nine, sir!"

"That's a shuttle bay. Why the hell would someone send him there?"

A strong vibration shook the deck.

Aubrey fell to his knees and laughed. Because someone wanted him to live at all costs. The only person who had known that there was no way in hell he could tap a Skeldhi ship.

Niobe.

He groaned. Bleeding Fate . . . What were they doing in Skeldhi space? Committing suicide. Niobe must have finally had enough of ship-killings and decided to take herself out of the game.

"Son of a fucking bitch!" The captain's shout came from dead ahead. "Give me the damned kid. You two get to battlestations!"

Aubrey felt his upper arm grabbed by a hand that had serious power in it. He was dragged to his feet and winced.

"Come on."

Aubrey went. There was no way he could fight the strength

in that hand. It would only get his arm broken. "I can't tap a Skeldhi craft. I don't have the programs."

"I know. The nav-pilot already told me."

Aubrey's brows shot up. "Then where are we going?"

"To your escape shuttle. Moribund will fry my ass if his most prized possession gets lost."

Aubrey licked his lips. "This would be a hell of a lot easier for both of us if I could see."

"Shit." The captain came to a halt. "Turn around."

Aubrey turned around. Something was jammed into his data port on the back of his skull, then yanked back out. The darkness brightened.

"Come on." The hand on Aubrey's arm jerked him back around and started hauling him down the hallway.

Aubrey squinted. "My sight is still offline."

"It'll get better. Your sight has been offline a while."

Aubrey clenched his jaw. "How long a while?"

The captain snorted. "Long enough to make you nothing but a scrawny bag of bones. I'm afraid if I sneeze too hard, I'll break you."

Aubrey was jerked to a halt. The hiss of an opening lift door came from right in front. Bodies moved past them. The captain pushed him into the lift.

Aubrey let himself be jerked around to face the front. "Captain, how long a while have I been a playing executable program floating in a liquid tank?"

The captain sighed. "Kid, you really, really don't want to know the answer to that one."

Aubrey clenched his jaw. "The men said nine cycles."

The captain chuckled. "It's been a little longer than that."

"How long?"

The lift doors opened. Smoke drifted into the lift with the sounds of screaming metal and shouting men.

Aubrey was shoved forward and angled to the left. His

eyes watered in the acidic air.

The captain leaned down to talk in his ear. "Just so you know, most of the docks have already been holed. I don't know how anyone knew to pull you from the tank and send you here, but this dock holds the one hidden shuttle on this ship. The first officer doesn't even know about it."

Aubrey choked. "You're abandoning your first officer?"

"Fuck yeah. It's a two-man craft. I'm taking the only thing Moribund wants to keep—you."

Aubrey shivered. "What the hell kind of people are you? Killing whole crews, even your own?"

"We're mercenaries."

Aubrey scowled. "That's crap! My dad was a merc and his company didn't do shit like that!"

The captain tugged Aubrey to a halt. "Yeah, well he didn't work for the Moribund Company, did he?"

Aubrey's eyes saw a colored blur right in front of him. He heard a door open. A hand at his back shoved him up some steps and through a door.

The captain followed right on his heels and grabbed his collar. "You know what Moribund means don't you?"

Aubrey grabbed for the hand at his collar. "No, I don't." He was propelled forward.

The captain chuckled. "It's an old Terran term for a dead or abandoned house."

Aubrey barked his shin on what he suspected was a chair. He hissed. "Appropriate since that's what you guys do, kill everybody on the ships to empty them."

"Pretty much." The captain shoved him into a chair. "Hold still." His hands closed around Aubrey's throat and squeezed.

Aubrey gasped and grabbed for his wrists.

The captain released him. "Relax, it's just a collar."

"What?" Aubrey grabbed for his throat and felt a metal ring around it. "What the fuck . . ." The ring went all the way around. He couldn't find a seam or an opening of any kind.

"Like I said, we can't afford to lose you. You've tripled our take since we jacked you in." The captain stepped away and a chair creaked to Aubrey's left. "Buckle in. This is going to be a bumpy ride."

Aubrey fastened the seat harness over him out of sheer reflex. "What the fuck did you put on me?"

"Oh, that's an old-style penal collar. It has a homing beacon in it. This way if we crash and you slip out of my hands, the ground party can find you anywhere on the planet."

"Wait a minute, we're over a planet?"

"Yep, but not much of one. The air's a little corrosive and you have bad lungs, so I'd stay on the ship if I were you."

The craft jerked hard under them.

"And we're away." The captain sighed. "Goodbye, *Interceptor*, hello raise."

Aubrey frowned. "Interceptor?"

"Oh, you didn't know? That's the ship's name."

"I thought it was Niobe?"

"That was its name when we got it. Sweet craft but a little unstable in places."

"Compared to what? Your nav-pilot is completely insane!"

"Yeah well, for a twisted little fuck, she could pull off miracles, and that's all that counted. We lost the occasional sub-pilot to her, but they were pretty easy to replace considering all the ships we took."

Aubrey gripped the armrests. "Do you even hear what you're saying? You are deliberately destroying people's lives!"

"So? What do I care? It's making me rich." The captain shifted next to him, flipping switches. "It's just the way the universe works kid, either you're predator or prey."

Aubrey folded his arms. "That's a total pile of shit."

"Hey, I'm not the one going back into a liquid tank at the

end of this trip to play subroutine to another ship."

Aubrey's temper flared hot. He shook with anger. "No, you're the one whose ship got blown all to hell because you wandered into the wrong territory."

"That was not my idea. The reason our asses got blown all to hell is because that damned ship shut down all external sensors and decided to pick a fight with the pilot. We didn't even know we were in Skeldhi territory and under attack until damage reports started coming in."

"Good for Niobe." Aubrey blinked and realized that he was seeing shapes. He could almost make out the dashboard right in front of him. He looked to his left and could just make out the hulking shape of a man next to him.

"You know, if I thought I could beat you without killing you, I'd do it."

"Like I'd care if you killed me? I'm going back into a liquid tank at the end of this trip remember?"

"Keep it up with the mouth, kid." The captain scowled, not a good look on his scarred and grizzled face. "I'm sure I can do something to make this trip really uncomfortable without breaking something."

Aubrey almost smiled. The captain's face might not be a pretty sight but his ability to even see it meant that escape was actually possible. *If it weren't for the fucking beacon collar.* Even if he did escape, he wouldn't get far. He licked his lips. But maybe he could get far enough to kill himself . . ."How long do we have until rescue?"

"What, change your mind about dying?"

Aubrey winced. *Shit . . .*

The captain grinned at him. "Ha, you did, didn't you?" He turned back to his controls. "Don't worry, it'll only be a matter of hours."

Hours? Aubrey sucked in a breath and choked. He only had *hours* to get far enough to die? The choke became a cough.

The cough became a spot of blood on his palm. He stared at in shock.

The captain nodded at him. "Oh yeah, there's a reason you were living in a tank kid. Without the nanites in the liquid to process oxygen for you, your lung problem is terminal." His smile was full of blackened teeth. "You can't breathe real air for more than a week or so. Your lungs were pretty much destroyed on your third trip to the airlock."

Aubrey turned to him in shock. "You knew about my being in the airlock?"

The captain shrugged. "Who do you think put you in it?"

Ice water filled Aubrey's veins; then his temper boiled white-hot. He fisted his cupped hand. For the first time in his life he really wanted to kill someone, and he wanted to do it with his bare hands.

Unfortunately, it was pretty damned obvious that the captain had marine-class robotic augmentation in his limbs. There was no way in hell that he could outfight or even outrun the bastard. He would have to find another way to kill him.

Chapter Four

The captain leaned back in the pilot's chair. "Moribund Company ships travel in threes; two next to each other, and the third, one jump behind, to pick up the pieces, if necessary. We had a terminal hit and the *Ravenous* was already dead by the time we regained outside sensors. The homing beacon on this baby will send the third ship, the *Ferocious* straight for us." The captain grinned. "You should be back in your tank by this time tomorrow."

"Great." Aubrey narrowed his eyes at the captain and then examined the blinking piloting controls. This craft was simplistic compared to the yachts he'd joyridden in. Maybe, he didn't have to escape. Maybe, he could kill the bastard in a crash.

And take himself out with him.

All he needed was some way into the ship's controls. Aubrey turned to look behind him. The craft was very small. The exit was directly behind them. The sleeping bays took up either wall with food service beyond the right bed and the facility beyond the left. He raised a brow. If this craft was like a few of the other small hoppers he'd borrowed, there was an engineering access panel in the floor of the facility. But how the fuck was he going to access it without a data-cable?

"Hey, kid?"

Aubrey turned to look at the captain. "What?"

The captain raised a brow at him. "You know how to fly one of these things?"

Aubrey blinked. It *couldn't* be that easy. "Well, yeah. I have limited piloting capability. Why do you think I was in that tank?"

The captain sneered. "Because you know how to break into them, the real question is, can you fly this one?"

Aubrey rolled his eyes. "Yes, I can fly this one. Why?"

The captain unbuckled his harness. "I have got to take a piss, and if you don't mind, I could use some sleep." He rose from the pilot's couch. "Once we get on the surface, we may have to deal with a Skeldhi hunting party or two. Not to put too fine a point on it, if you want to keep breathing, you're going to need me awake and aware to fight them off long enough for rescue to get to us."

Aubrey blinked. Fuck . . . It *was* going to be that easy. He smiled. "Sure, no problem."

The captain hesitated. His eyes narrowed. "Don't try anything funny, kid."

Aubrey set his chin on his hand and raised one brow. "What could I possibly do that you can't stop me from doing?"

The captain frowned.

Aubrey almost laughed. *Don't strain your brain, Captain.* "I'm not augmented remember?" His smile soured. "And I can't live outside a tank. If I don't go back in, I die in a week."

The captain smiled. "Actually, if you leave the ship, you'll be dead in a day or so. The atmosphere is slightly corrosive. No big deal for me, very big deal for you."

"Fine, you made your point." Aubrey unbuckled his harness. "Go take your piss and your nap." He climbed out of his chair.

The captain stood there, frowning.

Aubrey set his hands on his hips. "I only get to be outside a tank for a small amount of time. You have a problem with me enjoying what little time I get?"

The captain's expression eased into something almost like

regret. "Look, I'm sorry, kid, but it's your own fault you have to breathe water. If you'd agreed to the boss's deal when we pulled you out of the airlock the first time, you'd be sleeping in a captain's suite, not a tank. You're that valuable. Seriously, if I survive this without you, I'm a dead man."

Aubrey looked away and crossed his arms. *You just don't get it, asshole.*

"Tell you what, I'll see that you get out of the tank every once in a while so you can at least get laid."

Aubrey tilted his head and faced the planetary horizon line visible on the forward view-screen, turning his back on the hulking captain. "Sure, fine, whatever."

The captain sighed and turned away.

Aubrey dropped into the pilot's chair and activated the nav-pilot access. The mechanical feed at the back of the chair interlinked with his data-jack. Raw information poured into his skull. His imagination translated the data into stars and a slowly turning planet. It wasn't nearly as extensive as what a nav-pilot would see, but it was more control than the captain had, driving cold mechanics with his hands.

He crossed his arms and proceeded to plot his demise. He didn't bother to buckle in. The point was to ensure that he *didn't* survive the crash.

The small shuttle dipped below the planet's cloud level with the captain snoring up a storm in the bed directly behind Aubrey. Uneven rock-tumbled terrain spread beneath the ship. Patches of twisted trees and scattered hardscrabble bush seemed to be the only signs of life.

Aubrey tapped his finger on the armrest while piloting the ship closer to the surface. Death had to be really fast, or the captain would awaken and possibly stop the crash. He needed something to crash into, like . . . a mountain, if he could find one.

His sensors picked up a small craft unfamiliar in

conformation following his trail. It was not a Moribund ship or an Imperium craft. It had to be Skeldhi.

Aubrey's brows rose. Who needed a mountain when he could just get his ass blasted by an enemy ship? Oddly, something his father said a very long time ago came to mind. *The enemy of my enemy is my friend.*

He smiled and shifted the trajectory to make it easier for the other ship to catch him and shut down all the proximity alarms. The last thing he needed was the captain waking up and stopping him. He leaned back and set his hands behind his head while listening to the captain's loud snores. A smile played on his lips. Finally, all his misery was going to end, nice and fast.

The ship shuddered hard and whirled into a spinning curve that flung it from the other ship's path.

Aubrey grabbed for control. He needed to get back into that ship's path if he was going to make sure he didn't survive.

The captain rolled or rather fell from the bed. "What the fuck is going on?"

Aubrey rolled his eyes. "We have been hit by enemy fire and we are currently spinning out of control."

"Give me that!"

Aubrey was hauled from the pilot's chair and practically thrown onto the other chair.

"Go!" The captain dropped into the pilot seat. "Strap yourself in! I'll get us down in one piece."

Aubrey rose from the chair. *No, damnit!* He was going to crash this damned ship if he had to pry the engineering panel up from the floorboards with his bare hands.

The ship bucked hard.

Aubrey fell to the deck.

The captain choked. "Bloody fucking Fate! Where the hell did that come from?"

Aubrey grinned. Hot damn! They were under fire again.

The other ship had found them. Fate was finally smiling!

"What the fuck? The proximities are off! Kid, what did you do?"

"Who, me?" Aubrey rolled onto his back, tucked his hands behind his head and folded one knee over the other, kicking his foot absently. "Not a damned thing."

"Get your ass back in the chair! We're about to crash and crash hard!"

Aubrey smiled. "No thanks, I'm good."

"Are you trying to die?"

Aubrey rolled over onto his stomach and smiled at the captain. "Why, yes I am, you fucking moron."

The captain howled and climbed out of his chair. "Get in this chair, you stubborn little shit!"

Aubrey rolled up onto his feet and set his back against the door. He bared his teeth. "Fuck you!"

The captain grabbed the front of his ship-suit. "You will get in the fucking chair and strap in!"

In the forward view-screen, the mountain came out of nowhere.

Aubrey could not believe his good luck. "Um, captain shouldn't you be paying attention to that?"

"To what?"

Aubrey ginned. "The mountain, dead ahead?"

The captain looked over his shoulder. His mouth fell open and his eyes bulged.

Aubrey laughed. It was so perfect. Better than any comedy vid he'd ever seen.

The crash came blindingly fast. One second Aubrey was laughing in the captain's face and the next, he was being tossed around like a marble in a cup. The sound of ripping metal was horrendously loud.

Aubrey groaned. He was still alive. *Damnit!* He opened his

eyes and discovered that he was lying on top of the captain's rather large stomach. *Thanks for the soft landing, asshole.* And the captain was still breathing. He scowled. *Great . . .*

The air smelled bitter.

He looked up. A dark cloudy night sky was clearly visible over his head. The ship was a shredded mess all around them. He couldn't even tell what was supposed to be the deck and what was supposed to be the ceiling, especially the front. In fact, the entire nose, along with both chairs, was missing.

Aubrey smacked the closest surface with his palm. He should have stayed in the chair! He rolled off the captain's belly and climbed to his feet. He had a few small cuts and bunches of assorted bruises, but other than that, he was intact. Damnit. He eyed the litter lying about. There had to be something sharp enough to open his wrists or shove into his heart. He got down on his knees and started hunting.

Close to where the pilot's chair used to be, Aubrey found a fairly interesting and serrated shard of metal about as long as his forearm. Sitting back on his heels, he checked the edge. It felt sharp. He nodded. That ought to do the job pretty quick.

He turned the point to just below his breastbone and tilted it upward toward his heart.

An arm reached over his shoulder and a hand closed around Aubrey's wrists. "What the fuck do you think you're doing?" The captain's voice was right in his ear.

Aubrey ground his teeth fought to hold onto the blade of metal. "I should think it was pretty damned obvious."

"You are not committing suicide." The captain lifted the blade.

Aubrey came with it, hanging on with every drop of stubborn strength he had. "Yes, I am!"

The captain grabbed his shoulder with crushing force. "Let go!"

"You let go!" Aubrey jammed a foot between them, his

boot-heel catching on the larger man's upper thigh.

The captain gasped and suddenly toppled backwards.

Aubrey fell on top of him. Somehow in the fall, the point of the metal shard ended up in the side of the captain's neck. Blood welled and the scent of copper flooded Aubrey's nose. Rage bloomed out of nowhere. Aubrey pulled the blade from the captain's nerveless fingers, raised it, and plunged it down into meat and bone. Liquid rubies sprayed the air. He lifted the blade and plunged it down again, and again . . .

Aubrey sucked in a breath and tried not to cough. The chill air burned in his nose and seared every breath. The rocky ground was uneven under his unsteady feet. He was dead tired. The terrain was not exactly the most pleasant, just big towering rocks and twisted needle-leafed brush. He blinked watery eyes. He wasn't quite sure, but it looked like it was getting lighter. Was that dawn?

Aubrey dropped to the ground and leaned back against a large rock, staring at the dirty blade of metal that felt fused to his hand. The captain was dead. Very, very dead. Two hours walk away, dead. And it had felt so damned good to do it that he'd taken a nice little walk up the brush-covered mountain reveling in the feeling of finally defeating an enemy. He drew in another breath and coughed, and coughed, then spat a mouthful of blood.

His walk was finally over. It was his turn to die. He lifted the edged metal to his throat.

It clanged against the collar.

He winced. He needed to get that thing off or they would find him. He tilted his head to the side and pushed the metal sliver between his throat and the collar. He pulled. He pushed. He twisted. Warmth trickled down his throat. The sky turned an alarming shade of puke orange and rancid pink.

The collar stayed firmly around his throat.

Masculine voices spoke softly, very nearby.

Aubrey pulled the metal blade from his throat and climbed to his feet. He backed away from the voices.

Three grizzled men in ratty black and gold Moribund Company uniforms came around the edge of the rock carrying bolt rifles.

One of them frowned. "That him?"

Another looked at his hand. "That's what the beeper says."

The third held out his hand. "Come on, kid, time to go home."

Aubrey backed away and raised his hunk of metal. "Fuck you, I'm not going anywhere."

The third man took a step closer. "Kid you're going to be dead in two days."

Aubrey grinned. "You say that like it's a bad thing."

The second lifted his head. "What? Do you want to die?"

Aubrey bared his teeth. "Ask me if I want to live in a tank, asshole! Ask me if I like killing whole shiploads of people with the codes being raped out of my head!" He fisted his hands and screamed. "Yes! I want to die, you stupid son of a bitch!" He drew in a breath and choked. He grabbed his throat and started coughing . . . and couldn't stop.

"Stupid kid! This air is killing you!"

Aubrey caught a small breath and backed away, raising the blade. "Go away!"

"We should let him die."

"Moribund will kill us if we come back without him!"

"Shit."

The three men came toward him.

Aubrey turned and skidded down a small slope. There was no place he could hide. No matter where he went, they would find him. But maybe he could stay out of range long enough to die.

"Damned brat!"

"Don't let him get away!"

"He has a collar; he's not going far."

"Yeah, but we need to get him back in one piece, and still breathing!"

"Fine."

Aubrey crashed through the low brush and collapsed to his hands in a small clearing. His chest felt like someone was driving a knife into it and he couldn't catch his breath.

A youth in an iridescent black suit stepped out of the brush carrying a bolt rifle over his shoulder. His long ghost-pale hair was bound back in a tight braid that fell to his hips. The youth stopped and stared down at Aubrey.

Aubrey sat back on his heels and stared right back.

The youth was obviously Skeldhi. He had the sharply pointed ears and a sculpted face commanded by enormous blue eyes. He looked about half a head taller with broad shoulders on a sleek build. There was no way in hell Aubrey stood a chance against him, even without the bolt rifle in his hands.

The youth tilted his head to the side and frowned.

Aubrey scowled at him. "Well, what are you waiting for? Shoot me!"

The youth's eyes widened, and his mouth fell open. His gaze darted past Aubrey's shoulder.

"There he is!"

"I'll get the brat."

Aubrey turned sharply to look behind him. "Shit!" He lost his balance and fell onto his back.

The Moribund goon came straight for him.

Aubrey raised the hunk of metal with both hands. "Go away! Stay back!"

The man held out his hand. "Kid, come on, you'll be dead if you don't."

Aubrey lifted his blade and aimed for his own heart. "I know, leave me alone!"

The man took a step closer. "I can't do that. You're worth too much money."

"Oh, but you can." The voice was young, and gorgeously, inhumanly accented. A bolt shot echoed.

The Moribund goon gasped and fell back as though kicked in the head.

Huh? Aubrey looked behind him.

The white-haired youth lifted the nose of his smoking rifle and arched a brow. "You wanted him to go away, did you not?"

Aubrey felt a smile lift his mouth. "Yeah, I did. Thanks."

The youth grinned, showing long white predator's teeth. "It was my pleasure, truly."

The other two Moribund men shouted and came running.

The youth pointed his rifle and took them both out without even flinching. He walked over to Aubrey and held out a hand.

Aubrey stared at the bone-pale hand. *The enemy of my enemy is my friend.* He reached up and grasped his hand.

The youth lifted him onto his feet with hardly any effort. "I am Seht. And you?"

Aubrey took a small shallow breath to keep from coughing. "Aubrey."

Seht nodded and smiled. "Well then, Aubrey, shall we find somewhere else to be?"

Aubrey wrapped a finger around his collar. "They're tracking me with this. I can't get it off!"

Seht frowned. "I believe I can help." His gaze darted about. "But let us leave this exposed area first." He turned and started walking into the rocky scrub.

Aubrey stared after him bemused. *The enemy of my enemy is my friend.* Dad had it right on the money.

Seht turned back. "Coming?"
Aubrey nodded and strode after him.

Chapter Five

Seht led Aubrey uphill into the mountainous terrain. He looked back at Aubrey and pushed under some branches revealing the opening into a narrow path leading downward. "Your collar will lead them in this direction, but getting into this ravine is not all that easily accomplished."

Aubrey followed him through the brush and into the ravine's maze of narrow pathways. Feeling decidedly light-headed, he focused on Seht's gleaming white braid and the small pack on his back, his brain noting the rocky outcroppings and the twisted needle-leafed scrub enough to keep him upright, but not by much.

A rock rolled under his heel.

Aubrey dropped hard on his side and simply couldn't find the energy to get back up. He rolled onto his back and labored for breath.

Seht turned and frowned. "Aubrey?" He came and knelt at his side, setting the rifle down. "Are you wounded? I didn't think to check!" His fingers skimmed down Aubrey's legs and arms then across his chest. "No obvious broken bones, what's wrong?"

Aubrey smiled. "I'm dying."

Seht scowled, caught his arm and pulled Aubrey upright into a sitting position. "Of what?"

Aubrey crossed his legs, exhaled, and coughed. And coughed, and kept coughing, until blood spattered the ground beside him. "My lungs are bad."

Seht sat back on his heels. "So? Why did they not clone

another set and graft them in? Or give you nanite injections to repair them?"

Aubrey frowned at the puddle of blood next to him. He looked up at Seht and frowned. "I don't know. I've been in a liquid tank."

Seht's brows shot up. "For how long?"

Aubrey looked away and scowled. "Over nine cycles as far as I can tell."

"What?" Seht jerked back and fell on his butt. "But that is stupid!" He pushed back onto his knees. "A body cannot exist in a tank for more than three cycles before the body begins to adapt to the new environment."

Aubrey looked up at him. "What?"

Seht scowled. "Your lungs are not bad, they're incapable of breathing air that isn't liquefied! What did they put you in a tank for?"

Aubrey clenched his teeth. "They destroyed my lungs in an airlock."

"An airlock?" Seht's brows dipped. "I can see lung damage from such, but still, a liquid tank?"

Aubrey held Seht's blue gaze. "Try three trips in a row."

Seht blinked. "Three? In an airlock? Mother Night." A smile curved his mouth. "They must not like you very much."

Aubrey rolled his eyes. "What they didn't like was the word, no."

Seht's silver brows lifted. "No?"

Aubrey stared up at the roiling gray clouds. "No, I won't kill people, to be specific." He swallowed. "Not that it did any good. They hacked into me." He closed his eyes. "They used the contents of my head like a . . ." He took in a small breath, and it hurt. "I was slave-driven to their ship's sentience. I was a fucking subroutine the nav-pilot turned on when they wanted to take control of a ship, and then shut off when they were done." He leaned forward and hunched over his knees.

"They used me to take out a ship's life support, to kill the crews so the ship's sentience didn't suicide out of guilt."

Seht frowned. "*You* are the Moribund's ship plague?"

Aubrey chuckled softly and set his cheek on his upraised knees. "I guess you could call me that."

Seht raised a silver brow and a slight smile appeared. "You fought them I assume?"

"Constantly. Not that it did any good." He scowled and smacked the ground with the flat of his hand. "Once they got into my head, I couldn't get them back out."

Seht looked away, rubbing his jaw with his hand. "Aubrey, it seems to me that they deliberately made you a water breathing creature because a tank is the only way to maintain a hardwired body fairly indefinitely. You were being preserved, like a . . ."

"Like a what? Food?"

"I was going to say, a secret. Think, existing in a tank, you cannot speak to anyone but those that have direct access. Who is to know why you are there? Lock your tank in a dark room and no one even knows you exist."

Aubrey's eyes opened wide. "Only the ship and the nav-pilot had access to my head. The ship's sentience was my only contact. The nav-pilot was too freaking insane for any kind of direct mental communication. I spent a lot of time sleeping." When he wasn't being raped by the ship's sentience. "I don't even know how long I've been . . . doing this, for them."

"Aubrey, what is the last date you remember?"

Aubrey told him.

Seht frowned in thought, then his eyes opened wide. He scowled.

Aubrey frowned. "What?"

The pale youth looked away. "Grafting you a new set of lungs is not going to save you." He hunched his shoulders. "You are going to need genetic engineering."

"What?" Aubrey sat up. "Why?"

Seht looked up at the sky and sighed. "After a set amount of time, a human body in a water breathing environment adapts to the point that it cannot return to breathing air because every organ in the entire body adapts. You have been in the tank long enough to fully adapt." He winced. "And then some."

Aubrey focused on Seht's face. "How long?"

Seht turned away.

Aubrey grabbed for his hand. "Seht, how long was I in the tank?"

Seht looked down. "It takes one cycle to adapt to breathing water. It takes six for the entire body to adapt with it. It becomes irreversible after nine cycles."

"Seht, just spit it out." Aubrey tugged on the youth's hand.

"Sixteen."

Aubrey fell back onto his hands. "Sixteen? I reached majority ten cycles ago?"

Seht frowned. "Imperial legal majority? But you don't look anywhere close to that age!"

Aubrey snorted. "I was always a little scrawny."

Seht flashed a grin. "Scrawny is an apt description. You weigh no more than a child and appear to be at least four years younger than I. I am having great difficulty believing that you are actually older."

"I'm older than you?" Aubrey frowned. Seht looked awfully mature. His suit showed a lot of well-defined muscle, and he was clearly augmented, at least a little in his arms and legs. He had to be, to be so strong. "I'm older by how much?"

"By about . . ." Seht looked up at the clouds. "Six cycles I believe." He sighed and pulled off his pack. "Since you have decided that we shall rest here . . ." He flashed a smile. "When was the last time you ate?"

Aubrey grinned. "Sixteen cycles ago." His grin slipped

away. With his crew, in the mess hall, back on his old ship, fighting with the master engineer over sweet rolls. He closed his eyes. *Fate, they've been gone for over a year, nearly two.*

And in the past nine cycles he gave Moribund forty-seven ships. How many had he given them in sixteen? He was too tired to bother fighting the hurt. The tears fell silently. "You don't have to feed me. I'm dying."

Seht sighed. "You do not have to die if you do not wish to."

"I think it's better if I do. I can't go back to them. I can't chance that they'll get back into my head and kill more ship crews." He turned to look at Seht. "Promise me!" He grabbed for Seht's wrist. "Promise me that if they get me, you'll shoot me dead. Swear that you won't let them take me alive!"

Seht closed his warm hand over Aubrey's cold fingers. His eyes narrowed and heated to the bright blue heart of a flame. "No one will take you from me." His lips pulled back baring long vicious canines. "This I swear."

A shiver raced through Aubrey's body. He had absolutely no doubt that Seht meant every word. "Thank you." Relief spilled through him in a massive wave that became a sob. "Fate, I can't believe how much of a freaking baby I've become; blubbering for no apparent reason whatsoever."

Seht snorted and rummaged in his pack. "You do have reason. Grief is a reason. My half-brother, on the other hand, whines if his shoes are too tight." He held out a blue squeeze bottle. "Here."

Aubrey took the bottle. "What's this?"

Seht dug back into his pack. "A protein drink. I suspect that your stomach will not be capable of solid food."

Aubrey raised his brow and smiled sourly. "You think?"

Seht pulled out what looked like a sonic wrench. "Drink, I am going to see about removing that transmitter collar."

Aubrey upended the bottle and swallowed. The liquid was thick and strongly flavored, though not bad. "This has a weird flavor. What's it made from?"

"It's just a base vitamin protein liquid." Seht moved behind him and fingered the collar. "It tastes like plain water to me." He set his tool to the back of Aubrey's neck. "Considering that you have tasted nothing in sixteen cycles, perhaps it is not so unusual that you detect a flavor."

Slight vibrations shivered at the back of Aubrey's head. "If it's not supposed to have a flavor, and I'm tasting it, I can't even imagine how real food is going to taste."

Seht sighed. "Ah!" He tugged and the ring came apart. He pulled it from Aubrey's throat. "There!"

Aubrey turned around and grabbed for it. "Give me that!" He shoved onto his feet, threw the ring down, and slammed his heel down on it. "You stupid piece of shit, thing . . ." He slammed his heel down on it again, and again, his swears becoming more creative with each slam of his heel.

He dropped to his knees, out of breath. "Fate damned thing . . ."

Seht got up, picked up the ring and examined it. "Alas, I do not believe you have done it harm." He smiled down at Aubrey. "What do you say we throw it?"

Aubrey gasped for small breaths. "How far can you throw it?"

"Let's see, shall we?" Seht stepped back, lifting his empty hand, he pulled the hand with the ring back to his opposite side. He snapped his wrist. The ring flew spinning, outward and far down the mountain. He turned to grin at Aubrey. "That far."

Aubrey grinned. "Gee, I feel better already." Safe, he was safe. Finally. His vision closed down to a small point very far away.

"Aubrey?"

Aubrey fell over. The rocky ground was nice and soft against his cheek.

CHAPTER SIX

Warmth against his chest, soft skin under his hands and arms around him . . . Aubrey sighed and felt flesh under his cheek. This dream was more real than anything he'd experienced yet. "Niobe?"

"Aubrey?" The voice was in his ears, not his mind and it wasn't feminine.

The body under him had a heartbeat and breathed. It wasn't a dream. Aubrey opened his eyes to firelight and the interior of a small cave. He lifted his head and found himself staring into Seht's sleepy blue gaze. He was sprawled right on top of him. They were bare chest to bare chest with a blanket wrapped around them. It was actually pretty cozy; if a bit intimate. He felt his cheeks heat. "Um . . ."

Seht smiled. "You decided that it was time to sleep, so I found a cave to sleep in."

Aubrey winced. "I passed out on you."

Seht curled his arm behind his head. "That, too."

"Sorry." Aubrey moved his hands from Seht's bare chest and leaned to shift away.

Seht closed his other arm around Aubrey, holding him on top of his warm body. "Stay where you are, Aubrey. Go back to sleep." He closed his eyes.

Aubrey set his palms on the ground to either side of Seht's waist and felt some kind of air mattress spread under them. "You want me to sleep on top of you?"

Seht smiled but didn't open his eyes. "That is where I put you, is it not?"

Aubrey felt a stirring in his loins and knew he needed to be somewhere other than he was. Immediately. "I can sleep on the ground."

"No, you cannot. It is too cold, and the ground is much too hard for you."

"Seht, really, I can't sleep on top of you." His current position was too similar to the dreams Niobe had given him and his body wasn't noticing the obvious differences. He shifted to move away.

Seht closed both arms around him and raised his knees, trapping Aubrey between them. "Stay where you are, Aubrey."

Aubrey felt Seht's bare belly shifting under his. He frowned. How far down was his suit open? His cock began to harden. *Shit . . .*"Seht I really think I should sleep somewhere else."

Seht's hand slid down his back. "You do not sleep well anywhere but here."

"Huh?"

Seht opened one blue eye. "Put your hands back on my chest. You take a chill too easily."

"I'd rather not."

Seht sighed. "Aubrey, you have difficulty sleeping anywhere other than where you are. I would like to get some sleep myself. Please, put your hands back on my chest and go to sleep."

Aubrey winced and put his hands back on Seht's warm chest.

"Good. Now, lay your head down."

Aubrey set his cheek against Seht's chest. And stared at a stiff pale pink nipple. He closed his eyes and felt heat coiling into his cock. Very slowly, he twisted his hips to keep his swelling cock off Seht's belly.

Seht's hand pressed against Aubrey's butt, keeping

Aubrey firmly flat against his stomach. He sighed and rolled his hips, bringing one hell of an erection up against Aubrey's.

Aubrey stiffened and his eyes opened. "Seht?"

"Yes, Aubrey?"

"Um . . ."

Seht groaned. "Do not tell me you have never felt another man's cock before?"

Aubrey curled his hands closer. "Been in a tank sixteen cycles, remember? I hadn't reached majority yet when they put me in it?"

Seht trembled under him. The trembling became chuckles. "Are you saying that you are a virgin?"

Aubrey scowled. "It's not funny."

Seht threw his head back and howled with laughter.

Aubrey's cheeks flooded with heat. He pushed up angrily. "So, I've never fucked before." At least, not a living person. "Damn it, Seht, it's not a crime!"

Seht locked his arms around Aubrey and grinned. "No, it is not a crime, but I have been fucking for a good many years. It has been a very long time since I found a virgin older than myself!"

Aubrey scowled. "Seht, quit being a pain my ass."

Seht's smile turned predatory. "I haven't even begun yet."

The hair on Aubrey's neck stiffened in instinctive alarm. He didn't like that smile one tiny bit. Especially not when there was a very hard cock pressed against his. He shoved against Seht's chest. "Let me go."

Seht's grin disappeared and his arms closed tight around him. "Aubrey, stay. You do not sleep well anywhere but here."

Aubrey rolled his eyes. "Right." He pushed against the hard chest under his palms. "Seht, let me go."

Seht's eyes darkened and his mouth tightened. "Aubrey, please. I can't . . ." He closed his eyes and sighed. "Your nightmares tear at me. Please. You sleep quietly this way."

Aubrey stiffened. "Nightmares?"

Seht turned his head away. "I do not know what was done to you, but it makes you . . . weep."

The energy left Aubrey's body in a rush. He eased back down on Seht's chest, curling his hands in without thinking about it. He turned to face the fire. "They used me to kill the crews on the ships they took. They said forty-seven ships in the past nine cycles." He swallowed. "I have no idea how many in sixteen."

"You told me you did not do this willingly." Seht's voice was calm.

"I was hacked into. The nav-pilot accessed the programs out of my head to do it." Aubrey took a deep breath. "I was a subroutine to the ship's sentience."

Seht cupped a hand to the back of Aubrey's head, pressing Aubrey's cheek to his heart. "Who is this Niobe?"

Aubrey winced. "She was the ship's sentience."

"And?"

Aubrey closed his eyes and rubbed his cheek against Seht's soft skin. "I'd rather not say."

"Aubrey, you were shouting at her to stop and weeping. What did she do to you?"

"She, um . . ." Aubrey bit down on his lip. It sounded so stupid to say that you were raped by a ship's sentience. It wasn't as if it was done by a live person, even though it felt real enough while it was happening. The body count was certainly real enough.

"Aubrey, you are shaking." Seht's voice vibrated with a touch of anger. "What did she do?"

Aubrey's chest tightened. He shifted to his side a little and curled up as tightly as he could to hold the pain in. "It sounds so stupid."

Seht's arms closed around him, holding him in place.

"Whatever she did, it was not stupid." He sighed. "Tell me."

Aubrey closed his eyes tight. "When I fought to keep them out of my head, she used . . . sex to get in and take whatever they wanted."

Seht stilled then his arms tightened. "You were raped?"

"Yeah." Aubrey felt his heart burst in his chest. He grabbed his elbows to hold it in. "She didn't want to do it. She was so lonely, and I was the only friend she had. She would show me the stars she flew past." He barely felt the tears burning down his cheeks. "She knew she was . . . raping me. I could feel how much it hurt her every time she . . . did it, to get at what was in my head. She wanted to stop. She begged me to just let them take it, but I couldn't. I just couldn't. People died every time they used my programs."

Seht pressed Aubrey's head to his heart. "It's over, it's done. She's gone. The ship was dead before I found you."

"She did it on purpose. She came here, because I can't get into your ships. She had me pulled from the tank and sent to an escape ship. The captain found me, but I crashed the ship and he's dead. She came here to free me, and die." Aubrey shook as the sobs came tumbling out. "She killed herself for me. Everybody dies because of me."

"Aubrey, stop." Seht sat up and caught Aubrey's shoulders, trapping his gaze. "Listen to me. You did not kill those ship crews."

Aubrey shivered in Seht's grasp. "It was my programs . . ."

Seht shook his head. "That you did not willingly give."

Aubrey sucked in a small breath. "No, I didn't."

Seht's gaze hardened. "Think, if my brother were to beat me to the ground and take my gun from my hands, and then he went out and killed a hundred people with it, is it my fault that they died?"

Aubrey stilled. "No."

Seht raised his brow. "Whose fault was it?"

Aubrey frowned. "Your brother's."

Seht pursed his lips and tilted his head. "Say that he returns the gun to my hands, but then he wants to use it again. Say also, that I refuse to let him have it because I know that he intends to harm others with it, but he takes it from me anyway and kills more people with it. Is it my fault those people died?"

Aubrey frowned. "No, you didn't shoot them."

Seht raised his brow. "Nor did you."

Aubrey opened his mouth.

Seht pressed a hand to his lips. "No, Aubrey. You said no, and you fought to stop them. You did not win your fights, but you did not use that weapon to kill those people. The weapon was not in your control."

Aubrey scowled. "It wasn't supposed to be a weapon!"

Seht rolled his eyes. "In the hands of a skilled assassin, a sheet of paper can be a deadly weapon."

Aubrey's brows shot up. "A sheet of paper?"

Seht smiled. "Remind me to show you sometime." His brows lifted. "Now, who *really* killed all those ship crews? Who chose which ships to use that weapon on?"

Aubrey felt a knot of white-hot hate enfold his heart. "Moribund. He was the one that pulled me from my ship and killed everyone else. He ordered me sent to the airlock because I told him I'd rather die."

"Did you now?" Seht tilted his head. "That is who was after you, is it not? Those were his men?"

Aubrey nodded and scowled. "The captain said that I'm Moribund's most valuable possession."

Seht smiled. "I should think so. Your program made it possible to steal a great many ships. Without you, he will have to go back to his original method." He raised a brow. "What I do not understand, is why he did not simply make a copy of your program, and then kill you?"

Aubrey winced. "He probably has a copy, not that it will do him any good. The program is in my personal coding language." He glanced away. "When I was a kid I got hacked into at school." He shook his head. "It was for some stupid homework assignment, but it pissed me off, so, I invented a coding language of my own. I store everything in it. It switches to normal coding when it's activated, but without the keys, it won't activate. That's what Niobe was doing. When she . . ." He took a breath and released it. "They mapped me and found where the keys were stored, but they couldn't activate them. She would . . . make me cum and it would trigger the keys." He shrugged. "I still don't know why it worked, but it did."

Seht nibbled on his full bottom lip. "Climax is a full-body release. It may be as simple as that. When your body released tension, so did your mind."

Aubrey raised a brow. "How did you get so good at explaining stuff?"

Seht smiled. "When you are blamed for a great many things, you eventually learn how to rationalize just about everything." He leaned closer. "My uncle claims that arguing with me is like arguing with a bulkhead."

"I can see the similarities." Aubrey smiled. "My dad used to tell me I was too smart for my own good."

Seht snorted. "I can definitely see the similarities there."

Aubrey sighed. "So, now what do we do?"

"Now?" Seht closed his arms around Aubrey and pulled him down onto his chest. "Now, we sleep." He pulled the blanket up over them. "Hopefully you will rest this time."

Aubrey frowned at him. "You still want me to sleep on top of you?"

"Definitely." He closed one arm around Aubrey's waist and set the other under his head. "You may sleep under me next time."

Aubrey pulled his hands in. He was too exhausted to fight anymore. "If there is a next time." He took a deep breath and coughed and coughed. He leaned over Seht's side to spit the blood from his mouth.

"Aubrey, do you wish to live?" Seht's voice was very soft.

Aubrey stared at the blood on the ground. "I can't afford to let Moribund get me again."

"Aubrey, I have a way to save your life and keep Moribund from every touching you again. Do you want it?"

Aubrey settled against Seht's heart. "What? A mindwipe?" He considered it. It would stop Moribund from killing people, but everything he was would go with it. "I don't want my mind wiped. Better to just kill me. I don't think I could live with an empty head."

Seht took a deep breath. "No, I will not wipe your mind. You could stay with my people, with me."

Aubrey yawned. "As what? What could I do for your people? I don't even know the language."

Seht rubbed his palm across Aubrey's back. "As my personal consort."

Consort? Aubrey frowned. "Is that like, your lover?"

"Yes, and my friend. You would be part of my household."

Aubrey turned to look at Seht. "You're serious?"

Seht winced. "Is the idea of being my lover so awful?"

Aubrey thought about it. Seht was certainly attractive enough. His dick was still hard. Seht seemed to genuinely like him, and he liked Seht . . ."I'd have no problems being your friend, but I have no idea how to be somebody's lover."

Seht smiled. "It will be my great pleasure to teach you pleasure." He closed his arm around Aubrey's back. "Sleep, I will ask you again in the morning."

Seht's friend and lover. Aubrey curled his hands between them, feeling Seht's chest rising and falling under his palms and cheek. He smiled and took small shallow breaths. It was a nice dream, but every breath he took was a knife-blade saw-ing in his chest. He doubted he was going to be alive by morn-ing. It was probably better this way anyway.

CHAPTER SEVEN

His lungs stopped working.

Aubrey's eyes flew open. He gasped for breath and nothing entered. He couldn't breathe. His body shuddered then jerked violently. He couldn't breathe! Wind roared in his ears. Within his chest, pain began to slam, one hammer-blow after another.

Seht jerked awake, grabbed Aubrey's shoulders, and sat up shouting in Aubrey's face.

Aubrey couldn't hear him past the howling in his ears. Pain and panic squeezed his heart. He twisted sharply, falling from Seht's body to sprawl on the floor, writhing and gagging for breath.

Seht rolled from the bed after him.

Gasping, Aubrey rolled onto his side. He wheezed a tiny breath of air into his lungs and choked. Hot thick liquid exploded past his lips and scarlet splattered the sand.

Seht jerked back, scrambled to his feet and dashed off to his pack.

Aubrey rolled over onto his stomach and pushed up on his hands. He coughed hard. More blood spattered the sandy floor. Too much blood.

Seht dropped to his knees at Aubrey's side. He fumbled a smooth black case open on the floor and pulled out a long needle. In seconds he had a huge syringe filled with iridescent liquid ready in his hand. His mouth white and his eyes wide he shoved Aubrey onto his back and straddled his hips. Holding Aubrey down with one hand on his shoulder, Seht shouted. "Do you want to live?"

Aubrey blinked up at Seht. His vision began to fade down a long dark tunnel. He barely heard him.

Seht shook him hard. "Aubrey, stay with me! Do you want to live?"

Aubrey groaned and struggled to hear what Seht was asking.

"Aubrey, damn you!" Moisture slid from one huge blue eye and trickled down a bone-pale cheek. "Do you want to live? Yes or no?"

Aubrey frowned. What did Seht want? Moisture dropped from Seht's chin onto Aubrey's cheek. Tears. Aubrey felt a different pain grab his heart. Seht was weeping. Aubrey gathered what breath he could. "Seht . . ."

Seht wiped his wrist across his eyes and raised the syringe. "Aubrey, please! You're dying, right now!" His fingers dug sharply into Aubrey's shoulder. "Do you want to live? Yes or no?"

Aubrey struggled to think. Did he want to live? He hadn't had the chance yet. He'd reached majority in a tank. He hadn't even had his first real sex yet. Seht had promised he wouldn't go back, that he wouldn't let them take him. Tears streaked from his eyes. "Yes." It came out as barely a whisper.

Seht's jaw clenched. "Done." He slammed the syringe straight into Aubrey's chest.

Light exploded within Aubrey's heart. He didn't have the breath to scream.

Aubrey choked and rolled onto his belly. He spat and something small and hard flew from his mouth with a mouthful of copper-flavored liquid. He couldn't see past the tears in his eyes. "Shit . . ."

A hand rubbed his back. "Relax, you are shedding your human teeth."

Aubrey couldn't think. "What?" Exhaustion washed Seht's

reply from his mind.

Aubrey was held tight, cradled in a warm embrace. Something warm was jammed across his mouth and hot thick coppery liquid was pouring down his throat. He choked and then swallowed. A full breath raced into his lungs. He could breathe. Surprised, he opened his eyes and blinked up at Seht's face.

"Ah, awake?" Seht's mouth was tight and his eyes red-rimmed above him. "You are certainly a mess, pet."

Aubrey frowned. *What the . . .* He was cradled against Seht's right shoulder and sprawled across Seht's folded knees. Seht's wrist was jammed across his mouth, and Seht's blood was pouring down Aubrey's throat from an open wound slashed in his wrist. Aubrey could feel it against his tongue. He could also feel that some of his teeth were a lot longer than they should be.

Trying not to swallow, Aubrey pushed at Seht's chest and opened his mouth wide to pull his teeth from Seht's arm. He had no interest in drinking anybody's blood.

Seht pressed his wrist tighter to Aubrey's mouth. "Aubrey, don't fight, drink. Your body is starving for nutrients."

Aubrey swallowed to keep from choking, and warmth spread all through his body. An odd hunger bloomed. His lips closed on the open wound pressed to his mouth. He sucked.

Heat filled Aubrey's belly and spilled through him, bringing in a wave of mild euphoria. A soft moan escaped. The hunger became demanding. He bit down on Seht's arm and sucked harder. His thoughts pulled apart and sleep beckoned. His eyes drifted closed.

Seht sighed. "That's it, drink. You'll feel better very soon."

Aubrey's bladder forced him up off Seht's sleek, warm

chest. His open suit slid, falling past his hips. He grabbed for it and stumbled barefoot across the sand to the open mouth of the cave. The outer darkness was full of rain and rumbling.

Aubrey winced. If he stepped out there, he'd be soaked in seconds. But, damn it, he didn't want to piss in the cave . . . He scratched at his chest and looked down. His chest was covered in some kind of brown flakes. Blood. He was smeared with dried blood. Needed nutrients or not, he still couldn't believe Seht had insisted that Aubrey drink his blood. He shook his head, shying away from those thoughts. What he needed was a shower.

Aubrey looked at the falling rain, grinned and dropped his suit, stepping from it. He stepped out into the rainfall naked. Icy chill sluiced down his skin and soaked him thoroughly. He gasped in shock. It was fucking cold! He stumbled to one side to use the wall of rock by the cave mouth to relieve himself. His skin raced with chill. He scrubbed at his chest in the frigid rain and ran his fingers through his hair for good measure to get the blood off as fast as he could. He dashed back into the cave and shook off some of the water.

"Enjoy yourself?"

Aubrey looked over at Seht, folded his arms across his chest and shivered hard. "Oh, yeah, sure . . . In case you didn't know, it's fucking cold out there!" His words slurred just a bit. He explored with his tongue and discovered that his upper and lower canine teeth were longer than he remembered. A *lot* longer than he remembered. They felt like . . . fangs?

"Come here and get warm." Seht smiled and pulled back the blanket, exposing his pale, muscular chest. "You could have used a wipe if all you wanted was to get clean."

"I needed to ah . . ." Aubrey felt heat spread across his cheeks. "I needed the facility." He grabbed his suit and leaned back against the cave wall to get into it.

"I see." Seht frowned. "You're going to get your suit wet. Come, I have an extra blanket you may use to dry yourself." He turned and leaned toward his pack by the fire showing the long graceful line of his spine, and the curve of his bare backside.

Aubrey's brows lifted. Seht was naked? He spotted Seht's black suit, folded neatly by his pack. Seht *was* naked, and he'd been sleeping on top of him. A coil of erotic heat spilled downward. His cock twitched.

Aubrey winced. Terrific, just what he needed—a hard-on. He positioned his suit to hide his growing erection and walked cautiously toward the fire, and the bed. What was with him? He'd never had any real interest in guys before, but something about Seht was really getting to him.

Seht turned back over, leaning on his elbow as he held out a gray blanket. He smiled. "You are shivering."

"Thanks." Aubrey took the blanket from Seht's fingers and turned his back, dropping his suit to the sand. He dropped the blanket over his head to towel his wet hair. It had gotten really long, and it was dripping everywhere.

"I'll take that." Seht flipped Aubrey's suit over by the pack.

Aubrey froze.

Seht turned back over and smiled. "You won't need it till we leave the cave." The blanket slithered from Seht's hips revealing a pair of magnificently rigid erections, one right on top of the other.

Aubrey swallowed hard. Two, he had two . . .

Seht grinned. "You did not know?"

Aubrey sucked in a breath. "Um . . . no." He couldn't stop staring.

Seht rolled onto his back and gasped with laughter. "Chaos, you should see your face!"

Aubrey scowled. "Oh yeah, very funny!" He turned his back and scrubbed his skin ferociously, staring at the rain falling past the cave mouth. Like, he was supposed to know everything about all the other races? He knew that some of them were . . . paired. He just hadn't realized that Seht's race was one of them.

"Aubrey." Seht's voice was soft, and right behind him, only inches away.

Aubrey froze. His breath stopped briefly. He hadn't even heard Seht climb to his feet. Seht's hand pressed against his right shoulder, and the sensation burned straight down his spine.

"Turn around. I want to see you."

Aubrey turned, unable to resist the pressure on his shoulder. He faced the taller male and looked up.

Seht's bright blue eyes were full of heated interest. His silver hair spilled free down his creamy shoulders to his back, and his smile was carnal. "Oh, yes, you will do nicely. Sturdy frame, good bones . . ." His hands cupped Aubrey's shoulders, then slid up into his hair, his fingers tangling in Aubrey's dark waves. "Once you fill out, you will be quite magnificent."

Aubrey shivered, but not from chill, from heat. He could smell Seht's skin and his arousal. Aubrey was suddenly and painfully hard. He barely stopped himself from grabbing his aching cock. "Um, thanks, I guess."

Seht's brow rose and his smile broadened. "Aubrey, are you afraid?"

Aubrey's spine stiffened. "Who, me?"

Seht's gaze heated to blue flame. "Good." He leaned down and brushed his mouth against Aubrey's.

A small sound of shock slipped from Aubrey. *He kissed me?* The warm dampness of Seht's tongue swept across his parted lips. Curiosity overwhelmed surprise and he reached out to taste Seht. He tasted of fresh water and something . . . else. Something feral and interesting. He opened his mouth wider and sought Seht's tongue, stroking boldly to explore that interesting flavor more thoroughly.

Seht moaned softly and reciprocated with a strong foray into Aubrey's mouth. His hands slid down Aubrey's arms, tugging him closer.

The hot brands of Seht's cocks pressed against Aubrey's stomach even as his own cock pressed against the firm softness of Seht's belly. Need burned. He couldn't stop himself from rubbing against Seht's belly, and his cocks. It felt incredible. He groaned into Seht's mouth, and closed his arms around the taller man's waist, pulling him tight against him while pressed his hips closer. He rubbed with greedy hunger.

Seht broke the kiss, pulled back and smiled. "Ready for your first fuck?"

Fuck? Aubrey jerked back only to find that Seht had him locked in a firm embrace. He looked up at the taller man and sucked on his bottom lip. "Seht, I . . ."

"You have nothing to fear, Aubrey." Seht's smile broadened and his eyes narrowed to slits of blue flame. "I am quite experienced with virgins." Seht's foot caught on Aubrey's ankle and pulled.

Aubrey rocked off balance and gasped softly. Trapped in Seht's arms, he tumbled with him to the air mattress, landing on his back with Seht's hard hot body atop him, pinning him down. Seht's long silver mane spilled around their shoulders. Aubrey swallowed and stared up at Seht. "Right now?"

"Yes, Aubrey." Seht dropped his head, reached out with his pink tongue and flicked the tip across Aubrey's erect nipple.

Fire erupted in Aubrey's sensitive nipple and lanced downward in a lightning strike straight to his cock. "Shit!"

Seht's palm closed around Aubrey's cock as his tongue continued to tenderly torture his nipple.

Aubrey cried out, caught between the blazing sensations of

Seht's tongue and his hot hand.

Seht stroked upward, then down.

Aubrey's spine arched and he bucked helplessly into Seht's hand. Fire gathered at the base of his spine and his balls tightened with urgency.

Seht lifted his head and smiled. "I'm afraid that you are in great need of a fuck." He released Aubrey's cock. "And I am in great need to give it to you." He leaned to the left and pulled a tube from under the edge of the mattress.

Aubrey gasped for breath and seriously considered begging Seht to grab his cock again.

Seht sat up, removed the cap, and squirted a large dollop of gel on his palm. He grasped the upper and larger cock, smearing gel from base to head. He groaned and smiled.

Aubrey sat up on his elbows. Seht was greasing his prick? "What exactly are you planning to do?"

Seht snorted. "Surely you are not so much of a virgin that you do not know?"

Aubrey licked his lips. Seht was planning to jam that freaking huge prick up his ass? "Seht, I've never been . . ."

"Ass-fucked?" Seht rolled his eyes. "I believe that has already been established?" He closed the tube and set it to one side. He smiled. "Turn over onto your stomach."

Aubrey sat all the way up. "What for?"

Seht dropped his chin and raised a brow. "I need to prepare you for me."

Sweat formed down Aubrey's spine. "Seht . . ."

"Aubrey." Seht leaned close and pressed a brief kiss on Aubrey's lips. "I promise that I will be a most careful lover." He sat back and set his hands on his hips. "Turn over."

Aubrey darted a glance toward his suit and another toward the open mouth of the cave, and the rain sheeting past it.

"You may run if you like, but I assure you, you will not find the results pleasant." Seht's voice was soft but without remorse.

Aubrey stared at Seht. "You wouldn't . . ."

Seht's mouth tightened, his smile disappearing. "I most definitely would. I have injected your body with a nanite solution that is currently transforming your body. You need to be mounted before the next dose or the process will kill you."

Aubrey's breath left in a rush. "You . . . what?"

Seht's expression hardened. "I told you before that you needed genetic re-engineering to save your life."

Aubrey stilled. Seht *had* told him that. He'd also said he'd had the means to do it. He frowned. "But, sex?"

Seht nodded firmly. "What is currently in your body weakens your DNA structure. When I cum within you, my DNA will influence yours, making you a *rehkyt*, a hybrid, part human, part Skeldhi." His gaze narrowed. "One way or the other, my cock is going up your ass. The choice is yours as to how it gets there."

Aubrey flinched back, shocked. He couldn't believe Seht was threatening him with rape.

Seht scowled and turned away, his hands clenching into fists. "I would really, rather not use . . . force." He turned back his gaze focusing on Aubrey. "Please, do not make me."

Aubrey leaned back on his hands. "You really have to do this?"

Seht released his breath and smiled tiredly. "I promise it will not be completely unpleasant."

Aubrey winced. "That doesn't sound promising."

Seht rubbed his gel-slicked palms together and his lips lifted in a half-smile. "Turn over, Aubrey."

Aubrey took a deep breath and leaned to the side, then turned over onto his stomach. What had he gotten himself into this time?

CHAPTER EIGHT

Aubrey leaned up on his elbows, his belly and erection pressed to the air mattress below him with his legs spread wide.

Seht knelt between them, his warm thighs brushed the inside of Aubrey's knees.

Aubrey stared at the shadows on the cave wall cast by the small fire while listening to the rain outside, but all he could think of was that Seht was getting ready to jam his monster of a cock up his ass. He'd been looking forward to losing his virginity, but this wasn't exactly what he'd had in mind.

Seht's hot palms closed on Aubrey's inner thighs, just above his knees.

Aubrey jumped and a small sound escaped.

Seht chuckled. "Is that fear?"

Aubrey clenched his teeth. "No."

"Good." Seht's hands slid upward, to the bottom curve of Aubrey's ass. His thumbs pressed into the crease, parting his cheeks.

Aubrey shivered hard and hunched his shoulders. *Shit, shit, shit . . .*

"Tell me . . ." Seht's gel-slicked thumbs pressed low, framing the very base of his cock, the tips brushing under his balls. "How does this feel?" He massaged either side of the very root of Aubrey's shaft, right in the crease.

Heat and erotic tension slammed up Aubrey's spine and tightened in his balls. He gasped and dug his knees into the bed, his hips rising from the mattress. "Oh, fuck!"

"A good reaction I assume?" Seht's voice was clearly amused.

Aubrey tucked his head and sucked in a deep breath. His cock was one solid hot vibrating ache. He was incredibly close to spilling. "Um, yeah." His voice came out high and tight.

"Good." Seht's thumbs pressed closer to the tight bud of Aubrey's anus. "You are very ready. You will likely climax very quickly."

The hair on Aubrey's neck rose and it felt like the back of his head was about to explode. "No shit."

Seht's finger circled Aubrey's anus.

Aubrey stilled utterly.

Seht's finger pressed. "Push out, pet, push out hard."

Aubrey closed his eyes tight and pushed. His anus abruptly released tension.

Seht's finger slid within and plunged deep. "There."

Aubrey's eyes flew open. It was odd, but not uncomfortable, though it was incredibly embarrassing to have someone's finger up his ass. He frowned. It was also a little snug. "You have some fat fingers Seht."

Seht shifted his finger around, lubricating his interior. "Do I?"

Aubrey cringed. It wasn't unpleasant, but it was not something he was used to feeling. But what really bothered him, was that Seht's finger was nowhere near the diameter of the cock he'd watched him grease. "Are you sure that you can . . ." He swallowed. "Fit?"

"I will fit. You will adjust." Seht briefly pressed against something deep inside Aubrey's ass.

An almost electrical shock burned deep in Aubrey's balls and exploded all the way up his spine. His cock pulsed to a hardness he hadn't even thought he was physically capable of. Aubrey gasped in a deep breath and his hands clenched on the mattress. "Oh shit . . ."

Seht chuckled softly. "Oh, yes, you are very ready." He withdrew his finger.

Aubrey's breath left explosively, making a small sound that was almost a whimper. Whatever Seht had been pressing in there, had brought him right to the edge. He seriously considered begging Seht to put that finger right back where it had been.

Seht came up on his knees and leaned over Aubrey's back, setting his hands to either side of his shoulders. His cock brushed against the seam of Aubrey's ass, then pressed, a long, hard, and hot weight. He pressed a kiss to the base of Aubrey's neck. "I will be gentle."

Aubrey drew in a breath. "Fate, I hope so." He winced and bit down on his lip. He hadn't meant to say that out loud.

Seht chuckled softly. "You will find pleasure, I assure you." He closed his left arm around Aubrey's waist, pressing against his back while lifting his hips and ass. He reached back with his right hand.

Aubrey trembled, but he couldn't tell if it was fear or anticipation. The broad hot head of Seht's cock nudged against his anus, then pressed. He resisted, he couldn't stop himself. The pressure on his anus increased.

Seht breath brushed his shoulder. "Push out, pet, push out hard."

Aubrey clenched his hands into fists and dropped his head. He pushed. His anus spread and gave way, and then spread some more. Abruptly his ass engulfed the broad cockhead. Pain sizzled from his anus up his spine. He gasped and jerked forward. "Shit!"

Seht tightened his arm around Aubrey's waist, holding him where he was. "Easy, pet . . ." The long nails of his fingers dug into his hip. "Continue pushing."

Aubrey panted for breath and pushed. Seht's cock forged deeper, the shaft spreading him and filling him with mercilessly rigid heat. He groaned. "Fuck, you're big!"

Seht's other hand closed on his shoulder. "No, you are new." He pulled, and shoved further in, and then further in. His second and smaller cock nudged under Aubrey's balls.

Aubrey shuddered under the ruthless invasion, held tight in Seht's embrace.

Seht's hips pressed against Aubrey's butt. He groaned. "Yes, there, I am in." He slid his arm from Aubrey's shoulder down to embrace his chest and sighed in obvious enjoyment. "You feel like a hot tight fist around me."

Aubrey trembled on his elbows. There was a dick in his ass. A big, achingly hard, and white-hot dick in his ass. "You feel like you're splitting me in half." He glanced down and saw the blunt and purple head of Seht's second cock nestled under his balls. The shaft curved up to nudge against his cock. An erotic shiver raced up his spine.

Seht pressed his cheek next to Aubrey's. "You will find pleasure. Eventually." He shifted, rocking the rod jammed up Aubrey's butt.

Aubrey gasped. "Oh, fuck!"

Seht put his chin on Aubrey's shoulder and grinned. "We will get to that presently."

Aubrey panted and tried to hold very still. Bloody Fate, Seht planned to saw that thing in and out of his ass? "I don't know if I can take it."

Seht snorted. "You will take it."

"Wait 'til you have a dick up your ass!" Aubrey growled past his clenched teeth.

Seht pressed a soft kiss to Aubrey's brow. "You are the virgin, not I, remember?"

Aubrey stilled. A vision of Seht's pale, muscular body spread face down filled his mind's eye. His dick twitched in interest.

Seht's warm hand closed around Aubrey's cock and

caressed him.

Aubrey sucked in a deep breath and all thought fled his mind but for the feel of tight and stirring warmth around his cock. His hips jerked, his aching cock begging for relief in Seht's hand. The cock in his ass slid outward just a bit. The tightly stretched ring of his anus protested.

"Yes." Seht's voice was soft in his ear. "Push into my hand."

Aubrey groaned, wanting to feel more of Seht's hand, but movement made his ass ache. "It hurts."

Seht's hand stroked to the base of Aubrey's cock then slid up to the flared edge of his cockhead and held. "More?"

Delight burned across his lower back and tightened his balls. Aubrey barely held back a desperate whimper. "Yes, Fate, yes!"

"Push."

The threat of pain fought with the promise of release. Aubrey groaned and pushed into Seht's hand. The dick in his ass eased achingly outward even as carnal delight seared along his cock. He jerked back to thrust again and impaled himself hard on Seht's cock. The cock stretching his ass ached on reentry, but it also hit . . . something that sent a bolt of raw, agonizing pleasure all the way up his spine. A deep guttural moan exploded from his lips.

Seht groaned. "If you do that again, I may not be able to resist taking you more quickly than perhaps you would like."

Aubrey pushed forward, forging into Seht's hand. The delight of being gripped coiled through him. He slid back onto Seht's cock slowly. The return of delicious pressure drew a groan from him, but it wasn't nearly as good as what the quicker thrust had given him. He needed more.

Seht sighed in his ear. "Yes . . . oh, yes."

Aubrey licked his lips and braced on his elbows. He thrust into Seht's hand then pushed back a bit faster. Erotic fire fared from his dick and within his ass. He gasped under the wash of intense delight, sharpened by the burn of his protesting anus. That was it. That was what he wanted. He thrust and pushed back a touch faster. Then again, and again . . .

Against his back, Seht tensed and his breathing quickened.

His mind blank under a wash of raw carnal desperation, Aubrey hammered back against Seht. He was going to cum.

Seht's fingers brushed against the precum leaking from the tip of Aubrey's cock. "Ah . . ." He slid his hand low on Aubrey's cock, gripping him tight around the base. His arm closed crushingly around Aubrey's waist, jerking him to a halt. "Enough, pet."

Aubrey strained against him. He was so close! "No!"

Seht's arm tightened. His fingers made a constricting ring around Aubrey's cock, stopping the flow of precum. "Yes."

Aubrey's balls ached with the need for release. "Seht, please! I'm right there!"

"I know." Abruptly he pulled back and thrust. He thrust again, hard. And then again . . .

Aubrey shuddered under the barrage of scorching delight. He grabbed the mattress under him and strained to counter-thrust—and couldn't. Seht was holding him too tight. He groaned. If Seht would just let go, he could cum. "Seht, loosen up."

Seht drove into Aubrey with punishing force. "No."

Aubrey threw his head back, groaning under the blinding pleasure and building pressure. "What are you doing?"

"I am fucking you, Aubrey."

"Damn it, Seht!" Desperation laced Aubrey's voice. "Let go! I'm right there!"

Seht wound his fingers into Aubrey's hair and jerked his head up. "You will cum when I am ready to let you."

"What?" Aubrey winced. "Seht, stop playing games!"

"This is no game, pet." Seht's lips, then the points of his

long teeth grazed the straining cords of Aubrey's throat. "Do you yield?"

The hair on Aubrey's body rose in alarm. The question sounded suspiciously ... permanent. "Seht? What's going on?"

"Answer the question." A growl rumbled from Seht's chest. He ground his cock deep into Aubrey's ass. "Do you yield?"

Aubrey trembled hard, desperate for the release Seht was keeping from him. "Seht, please ..."

"Do you yield?"

Aubrey's temper flared white-hot. Impaled on Seht's cock, a snarl exploded from his throat. "Fuck that shit!" He grabbed for Seht's hand around his dick, and the hand in his hair, scrabbling to get his feet under him. "Get off me!"

Seht jerked him up by the hair, off his hands and onto his knees. "Yield, damn you!"

"No fucking way!" Aubrey twisted hard and bucked to throw Seht off.

Seht's hand closed crushingly around his dick. "You *will* yield to me!"

Pain slammed the breath from Aubrey's lungs. He choked and his knees gave out. "Shit, shit, shit ... fuck!"

"You cannot win, Aubrey. Yield."

"Why, Seht?" Aubrey panted for breath. "Why is this ... so damned important?"

Seht's body tensed around Aubrey. He took a deep breath. "I will not have you killed, not after I saved you."

Aubrey froze, stunned. "What?"

"Aubrey, a *rehkyt* that cannot be mastered is destroyed."

"Mastered?" The word took Aubrey's breath away. "Seht, what the hell is going on here?"

Seht took a deep breath. "You must yield, to acknowledge that you are ..." He took a breath and released it. "That you agree to being my personal property."

What . . . Aubrey struggled to find another meaning for Seht's words, but they insisted on adding up to only one definition. Aubrey closed his eyes and betrayal burned in his heart. "Seht, I won't be your . . . slave."

Seht growled. "Aubrey, it is the only way to keep you from death."

"Fine, then let me die!" Cool moisture struck Aubrey's back. He turned and caught the gleam of tears streaking down Seht's cheek. The sight shocked him to the core. *Bloody Fate . . .* Seht was weeping?

"I will *never* let you die." Seht snarled, the sound boiling from his chest in a vicious spitting roar. *"Never!"* His mouth opened wide, baring his long fangs. His head dropped, burying his teeth deep in the meat of Aubrey's left shoulder.

Pain ripped into Aubrey's shoulder. He shouted in shock.

Seht's liquid growl vibrated through Aubrey's body and down his spine. He withdrew his fangs. "You will yield, damn you!" He stroked the wounds with his tongue.

Aubrey hissed in a breath. His tongue was not making it feel better. "What the fuck was that for?" Sensation exploded then rolled through him in a wave of pain, followed by brutal erotic heat. He gasped.

"Your resistance is done." Seht lifted Aubrey from his lap and dropped him hard, impaling him on his cock.

Seht's sudden possession induced a second wave of overwhelming erotic heat that washed through Aubrey in a molten wave of raw lust. His back arched and he shouted.

Seht shoved Aubrey forward onto his hands. "You will yield, and you will live." His fingers knotted in Aubrey's hair, holding his head up even as his arm coiled tight around Aubrey's hips. He thrust hard and fast, grunting with each powerful stroke, taking him without mercy.

Aubrey howled, his body shaking under the repeated

impact, writhing in erotic torment. The pressure in his balls and cock became a white-hot fire up his spine.

Seht growled in his ear. "Now, do you yield?"

His mind seared clean of all thought but the overwhelming and horrific urge to cum, Aubrey screamed. "Yes!"

"Yes!" Seht twisted his hips sharply.

Aubrey felt something round and hard shove painfully past his anus and into his body. He gasped in shock.

Seht pulled Aubrey upright spreading his thighs wide across his lap. His hand cupped Aubrey's balls, then he stroked the shaft firmly. "Cum for me, Aubrey."

Seht's strong caress was a burning pleasure that was far too close to pain. Aubrey threw his head back onto Seht's shoulder and howled. Climax exploded in a burst that seared up the back of his skull. Boiling hot cum slammed from his balls into his shaft and shot forth in a thick spurting stream. His back arched with a pleasure so intense he couldn't bear it. He shrieked.

Seht clutched Aubrey's shaking body, bucking hard up into him, and howled.

Aubrey felt the cock in his ass pulse. Cum spurted from Seht's second cock, spraying upward in thick hot streams that coated Aubrey's balls, cock and belly. He groaned and twitched with strong aftershocks.

He was well and truly fucked.

CHAPTER NINE

Seht rolled them to the left. Exhausted, they fell onto the sleeping mat, landing on their sides. Seht groaned and embraced Aubrey, tucking up his knees, spooning against Aubrey's sweat-soaked back, his cock jammed hard and tight in Aubrey's ass. His breath feathered the back of Aubrey's neck. "I swear I will take very good care of you."

Limp with exhaustion, Aubrey panted for breath. "Seht, I don't want . . . I want . . . to take care of . . . myself."

"I have not been impressed with how well you have been taking care of yourself to date." Seht's lips brushed his shoulder. "I will be good for you."

"That's not the point!" Aubrey shifted and winced. Seht's cock was lodged painfully tight in his ass. "I don't believe you're still hard."

"The base of my dicks knot. Eventually, they will loosen." His hand slid down Aubrey's belly. "It is to hold our mates while we ejaculate. The females of my race are very fierce even during their . . . season."

Aubrey frowned. "Your women have a season?"

"Oh, yes. Every two years, they go into compliance, for sixty days." His fingers brushed against Aubrey's cock. "Alas, we males do not share their season. We are ready at all times."

"Wait a minute, you can go for sixty days, but you only get to do it once every two years? That has got to be frustrating."

"Yes." Seht chuckled sourly. "It is."

Aubrey felt a smile curled his lip. It certainly explained why their race was so warlike.

"Which is why *rehkyt*, human hybrid concubines are necessary." Seht curled his palm around Aubrey's shaft. "It eases the . . . needs of the body."

"Great, just what I always wanted to be, a concubine." Heat coiled at the base of Aubrey's spine, and arousal stirred in his cock. He sucked in a startled breath and groaned. "Bloody Fate, I didn't think I'd be able to get back up again for a week."

"You are *rehkyt*. Your physical needs are designed to equal mine."

"Shit! You mean I'm going to be able to . . . fuck for sixty days straight?" Aubrey turned to look back at Seht.

"Fear not, I will satisfy your needs." Seht smiled, showing his long teeth. "And I will teach you to satisfy mine."

Aubrey groaned. "Why does that sound like a threat?"

Seht caught Aubrey's chin, encouraging him to turn and look at him. "You may consider it such." His mouth took Aubrey's in an aggressive kiss, his tongue surging in to take possession.

Aubrey's senses reeled under the assaulting caress.

Seht released his mouth and curled his arms around Aubrey, his palms brushing his chest with the long nails of his fingers brushing Aubrey's small hard nipples.

He moaned, his body surrendering to Seht's touch to bloom to full heavy erection.

Seht's lips brushed Aubrey's ear. "Now then, I ask you a question. The right answer gives you pleasure. The wrong answer brings you pain. Understood?"

Aubrey frowned. What the hell was Seht doing now?

"Do you understand?" He slowly pinched Aubrey's nipple between his long nails.

The pleasure was so intense it was, in fact, painful. Aubrey gasped. "Shit, Seht!"

"The correct answer is 'yes, '*Syr*.'"

'*Syr*? Aubrey sucked in a harsh breath. "Are you serious?"

Seht pinched his nipple again, harder. "Very."

Aubrey bit back a shout and groaned. "Son of a bitch, that hurts!"

"What is the correct answer?" His fingers hovered over Aubrey's aching nipple.

Aubrey froze in alarm. "Alright fine, yes, *'Syr!'*"

"Close enough." His hand gently caressed Aubrey's nipple.

Warm curls of delight rolled straight down to Aubrey's cock. He moaned.

"To whom did you yield?"

Aubrey stilled.

Seht's finger brushed his nipple in warning. "Aubrey?"

Aubrey couldn't stop his flinch. "You."

Seht's nails tapped his nipple with a long nail. "You, what? Say it properly."

Aubrey clenched his jaw. He didn't want to get pinched again. Seht had already proved beyond a shadow of a doubt that he was more than capable of making him scream. "You, *'Syr.'*"

"Very good, pet." Seht's palm swept across Aubrey's nipple.

Aubrey's cock pulsed in delighted but insistent appetite. He exhaled sharply. He couldn't believe he'd gotten this hard, this fast.

"Whom do you serve?"

Aubrey felt a low growl vibrating in his chest. "No one."

"Wrong answer!" Both nipples were pinched.

Savage pain erupted in Aubrey nipples. He shouted.

Seht growled. "Again, who do you serve?"

Aubrey barely heard him through the angry throb in his nipples. "Damn it! Seht!"

"Say it properly *rehkyt*." Seht's fingers long nails closed around Aubrey's nipples.

"You, '*Syr*.'"

"That's right." His palms swept across Aubrey's chest and down his belly.

Aubrey leaned back against Seht and moaned. Seht's touch soothed the angry ache in his nipples while making his dick ache for relief.

"Who do you want to serve?"

Aubrey stilled. He didn't want to serve anybody, but he absolutely did not want to get pinched again. "You, '*Syr*.'"

"Excellent." One hand slid down his belly to curl his fingers around Aubrey's aching cock. "And how will you serve me?"

Aubrey racked his brain. "I have no idea how to answer that."

Seht stilled.

Aubrey felt his heart beat in his mouth. If Seht squeezed his dick, the agony would make him scream. He grabbed Seht's wrist. "Seriously, I haven't got a clue here!"

Seht released a breath. "Try the word, obedience."

What? Aubrey's mouth fell open. He could feel felt the gap yawning under him. "Please tell me you're kidding?"

"I am not."

Aubrey's heart beat painfully in his chest. "Seht, I can't give you that . . ."

"You will give it." Seht growled in Aubrey's ear. "That you survive means more to me than your stubborn pride, Aubrey. Do not think I will not make you writhe in agony to get the correct responses from you. Again, how will you serve me?"

Aubrey's heart ached. He had trusted Seht. It wasn't fucking fair! He closed his eyes. "Damn it, I thought you were my friend."

Seht sighed and spoke softly. "Aubrey, your life means more to me than merely . . . friendship." A growl entered his voice. "I will do whatever is necessary to keep you alive." He took a deep breath. "Answer the question." His fingers closed around Aubrey's cock with clear intent.

Aubrey dropped his head and felt a vise close around his heart. A small sob lurched in his chest and tears spilled down his cheeks. He didn't want to say it . . . Didn't want to say it. . . . Didn't want . . ."With obedience, *'Syr.'*"

Seht released a breath and relaxed his hold on Aubrey's cock. "Blood and Chaos you are stubborn!"

Aubrey wrapped his arms tight across his stomach. "Is it over?"

"This is." Seht groaned and pulled back. His cock slid free from Aubrey's ass in a wash of wetness.

Aubrey flinched. The scent of Seht's cum was strong, and it was all over him. He didn't want to think about how badly he'd wanted to be fucked. He definitely didn't want to think about the fact that his body wanted more, and soon. His erection throbbed in time with his heartbeat.

"Aubrey, roll onto your back."

Aubrey rolled onto his back and winced. His butt *hurt*. He came up on his heels to ease the ache in his ass.

Seht stepped over him, straddling his hips. He held a massive syringe. "It's time for your second nanite dose."

Aubrey couldn't stop his lip from curling or the growl that rolled in his chest. "And my next fuck?"

Seht dropped down to sit across his hips. The pale shafts of his semi-erect cocks pressed against Aubrey's belly. "Yes." He set two fingers at the base of Aubrey's sternum and placed the long needle between them, angled to go into his heart. "Hold very still and take a deep breath." He looked down at his fingers.

Aubrey fisted his hands at his sides and took a deep breath, his chest rising under Seht's fingers.

Seht glanced at him. "Good. Let your breath out, slowly."

Aubrey began to let his breath ease from his lungs.

Seht punched the needle in, hard.

The pain was sharp and immediate. His breath escaped on a groan. Heat swelled within his heart and burned, spreading like molten lava through his blood with every heartbeat. His body felt like it was swelling under his skin. His brain caught fire, and then his heart was engulfed by a minor nuclear explosion.

Aubrey jerked awake. Time must have passed. He was soaked in sweat and had a raging hard-on that throbbed painfully in time to his aching heart. His thighs and the mattress under him were sticky with cum. There was no mistaking that he had been thoroughly fucked. He sucked in a slow breath and turned to look for Seht.

Seht knelt only inches away sucking on a squeeze bottle of what looked like a nutrient drink. He wiped his mouth with the back of his hand and scrubbed his hand through his long silvery hair. There were dark circles under his half-lidded eyes.

Aubrey frowned. "You look like crap."

Seht flinched just slightly, then a tired smile appeared. "I feel like crap." He rubbed his eyes. "Fighting your stubborn will is exhausting." He sighed. "I simply do not comprehend your complete devotion to dying."

Aubrey sighed and looked up at the arching cave wall above him. "Seht, there really are fates worse than death."

Seht growled and leaned over Aubrey, setting his hands to either side of Aubrey's shoulders. His lip curled, showing a long tooth. "I intend to give you a life of leisure very far away from Moribund's reach. How can that be a fate worse than death?" His scent, rich and arousing filled the air between them.

Aubrey took an instinctive breath to draw in more of Seht's delicious scent. He smelled so good. "I don't want to be given anything. I want to do it myself." He leaned up on his elbows and took a deeper breath. *That scent . . .*

Seht leaned closer, less than a kiss away and whispered. "Why struggle, when there is no need?"

Aubrey's complete attention was taken by the perfume of flesh and masculine arousal. Seht smelled delicious and intoxicating. He tilted his head and stroked Seht's bone-pale throat with his tongue, tasting sweat and arousal. Seht's pulse throbbed under Aubrey's tongue. Aubrey opened his mouth wider to taste more. His long teeth grazed pliant flesh.

Seht sucked in a groaning breath and fisted his hand in Aubrey's hair to jerk Aubrey's head back from his throat. He smiled. "It seems that your fate has been thoroughly decided. You've taken an impression."

Aubrey grabbed Seht around the shoulders and pulled, jerking the pale young man down onto the air mattress.

Seht grunted, his eyes opening wide.

Aubrey rolled over him and rose, framing Seht's with his hands. "Is that supposed to mean something?"

Seht smiled and his eyes narrowed. "Yes." He grabbed Aubrey's head and pulled him down into a searing, and thorough kiss.

Aubrey groaned and trembled. His body flushed with heat and urgency. Something very like a whimper escaped his throat.

Seht lifted his leg and shoved, knocking Aubrey onto his side, then rolled on top without releasing his mouth.

Aubrey didn't fight him. He didn't want to fight him. He dug his heels into the mattress and pushed up, rubbing his inflamed cock against Seht's smooth belly.

Seht groaned and pushed up on his knees, spreading them wide and shoving Aubrey's knees up and apart.

Aubrey trembled hard. Seht was getting ready to fuck him.

Seht pushed Aubrey's left knee up until his calf rested on

Seht's shoulder. He reached down with his right hand and pressed two fingers against Aubrey's anus.

Aubrey grunted, startled, but it wasn't painful. His body opened without any effort at all, and Seht's fingers slid into his body without any resistance.

Seht broke the kiss and smiled. "This time, you will feel only pleasure." He turned his hand, his fingers arching upward, and pressed something painfully exciting within.

Aubrey arched, gasping and his cock jerked, spilling just a tiny bit of cum. Toes curled tightly, he shook. He'd very nearly cum.

Seht pulled his fingers free and shifted. The broad, blunt head of his cock pressed against Aubrey's anus, while something else, just as hot and rigid slid between his ass-cheeks. "Ready?"

Aubrey sucked in a breath. Seht's larger primary cock was about to enter his ass. He was feeling Seht's secondary cock under him. *Crap* . . . He stared up at Seht, trembling from a potent and confusing cocktail of fear and anticipation. "Do I have to be ready?" His voice came out only a little tight.

"No." Seht shoved, entering hard and fast, pressing deliciously past that spot within Aubrey to slam all the way in.

Aubrey cried out and arched, his other knee coming up in sheer shocked reaction. "Fuck!"

Seht caught the raised knee then shoved both of his legs forward until Aubrey was curled up with his knees very nearly against his chest. Fully seated within Aubrey's ass, he leaned down and planted his hands on the mattress. "Precisely."

Aubrey swallowed and stared up at Seht. With his legs hooked over Seht's arms and his feet in mid-air, his body filled with painfully rigid heat, he couldn't move at all. His cheeks heated furiously, betraying just how embarrassingly vulnerable he felt.

Seht leaned down to deliver a sweet gentle kiss, and ground deep into Aubrey's ass, pressing deliberately against that hot point deep inside.

Hot, thick, cum slid deliciously into his shaft pressing against Seht's belly. Aubrey tensed and gasped into Seht's mouth, grabbing for the other man's wrists. "I'm going to . . . I'm going to . . ."

Seht's lips twisted into a sadistic smile. "No, you may not."

Aubrey's body locked up on him. He jolted in shock, his eyes opening wide. A startled cry left his lips before he could stop it.

Seht brushed his lips against Aubrey's cheek. His chuckle was barely a breath. "Good pet."

Aubrey groaned and flexed, his feet flailing, but in that position, he didn't have one ounce of leverage. "You . . . bastard!"

Seht's gaze narrowed and his mouth tightened. He pulled back and slammed in hard, pressing violently against that hot point within.

Intense and brutal pleasure knotted within Aubrey. His toes curled and a cry was forced from his lips.

"That is not how a pet asks for what he wants from his master." Seht ground into him, riding hard on that viciously sweet spot.

Aubrey howled.

CHAPTER TEN

Up on his widespread knees with Aubrey's legs hooked over his arms, Seht held perfectly still. His cock was buried deep in Aubrey's body and pressed viciously against that hot spot. He stared down at Aubrey and his lips curved into a completely ruthless smile. "Tell me what you want, pet."

Aubrey stared up at him, panting, his head and shoulders enveloped in the curtain of Seht's long white hair. His heart hammered in his chest and his body wouldn't stop trembling. His painfully hard cock dribbled onto his belly. He was desperate to cum and unable to do a thing about it. He clenched his jaw. He didn't mind asking, but he didn't want to say that word: 'Syr.

Seht's gaze narrowed.

Crap . . . Aubrey dug his nails into Seht's wrists. "Seht, you've got my body, okay? What more do you want?"

Seht's lips tightened into a thin line. "If you are to live, I must have your complete submission."

Aubrey swallowed. "Just how 'complete' are we talking here?"

Seht licked his lips. "I have your body, but I do not yet have your stubborn will."

Aubrey shifted uneasily. "I don't think I can do that."

"You do not have a choice." Seht's blue gaze brightened with moisture, but his lips curled back, baring his fangs. "I will have your submission so that you may live."

Aubrey's heart twisted painfully. "Why? Why do you want me to live so damned much?"

"Damn it, Aubrey . . ." Seht bowed his head briefly then tossed his head back up, flipping his long hair back. His gaze focused and heated. "Aubrey, I need you to live because . . ." He took a shallow breath. "I do not believe my sanity would survive your death." A single tear slid down his cheek. "I strongly suspect I may have actually fallen in love with you."

What . . . Staring at Seht's tear, Aubrey shivered. Was that why his chest hurt so badly? Was this love? *Shit . . .*

Seht leaned slightly to the side and lifted his hand to wipe at his damp cheeks. "Strange emotion, this love." He smiled briefly, and another tear slid down his cheek. "I'd always heard that it was glorious and uplifting."

Aubrey nodded. He felt like total crap. "They lied."

Seht choked on a small laugh, but his smile was only fleeting. "Indeed, they lied." He sighed.

Aubrey looked away. It hurt too damn much to see Seht's tears. "Damn it, Seht . . ."

"Aubrey, please . . . If I do not succeed in mastering you . . ." Seht's voice broke. "I will be forced to destroy you."

"You?" Aubrey stiffened, shocked. "Why you?"

"I made you." Seht sucked in a deep breath. "I am responsible for your existence. If I cannot gain your submission, I must destroy you." He pinned Aubrey with a glare and curled his lip, baring his long teeth. "If you force me to kill you, I swear I will follow you into death and torment you throughout your next life!"

Aubrey blinked. "You believe in reincarnation?"

Seht snarled. "My religion is not the point here, damn you!" His tears dropped onto Aubrey's cheek. "The point is, if you die, I die with you!"

Aubrey stared. He couldn't actually be serious? "You wouldn't . . ."

Seht spoke through his clenched teeth. "I most certainly would."

Aubrey's heart slammed in his chest. "That's crazy!"

Seht snorted and rolled his eyes. "I believe I just finished mentioning something to that effect?"

Aubrey's stomach did a slow, sickening turn, and his heart burned. "Seht, you can't mean that."

"I can, indeed." A blood-curdling smile graced Seht's lips, but his eyes shifted into ice blue feline slits. "And I more than have the means, believe me."

Aubrey dug his fingers into Seht's wrists, his heart beating in his mouth. "You can't die because of me." Too many had died already.

"And why not?" Seht's gaze narrowed. "If you can escape into death, I see no reason why I cannot follow you."

"You can't because . . ." Aubrey floundered for something to argue with, but not a damned thing came to mind. He simply could not stand the idea of Seht being dead. "Because you just . . . can't! All right?"

"Not good enough!" Seht bared his teeth. "And why should you care if I die? You'll already be dead!"

Aubrey shouted in his face. "Because I do care, you sadistic asshole!" A hot tear escaped down his cheek.

Seht stared, his eyes wide. "Aubrey?"

Aubrey blinked hard, but for some reason, the tears wouldn't stop. "What?"

Seht's mouth relaxed into a slight frown. "Do you . . . love me?"

Aubrey glanced away. He'd already opened his big, fat, mouth. There was no denying it now. "Probably."

"Aubrey, look at me."

Aubrey turned to face Seht's damp and burning gaze.

"You do not want me to die?"

"Yes. No!" Aubrey shook his head in confusion. "No, I don't want you to die."

Seht bared his teeth and shouted. "Then submit and *live,*

you stubborn bastard!"

Aubrey shouted right back. "Fine! I'll live!" He froze, shocked at his own words. He took an unsteady breath. "Ah fuck . . . This is blackmail, you shit."

"And your point is?" Seht smiled and a fresh tear streaked down his cheek. "Now, say it again properly, pet."

Aubrey winced. *Fate, did he never let up?* "I will live, '*Syr*." He bared his teeth. "And this is blackmail, '*Syr*."

Seht groaned. "Thank the Mother . . ." He dropped forward and took Aubrey's mouth in a fierce kiss that sucked the breath from his lungs.

Aubrey moaned and found something other than Seht's wrists to hang onto, Seht's shoulders worked beautifully.

Seht released Aubrey's mouth and pressed his forehead to Aubrey's brow. "You are the most exhausting *rehkyt* I have ever known."

Aubrey groaned and shifted under him. "Yeah, well being curled up with my knees at my ears and your dick up my ass isn't exactly relaxing." He let go of Seht's neck to wipe at his burning eyes and smiled. "Can we fuck now?"

Seht raised a pale brow. "Was that a question?"

Aubrey rolled his eyes. "Oh, for bleeding Fate . . ." He narrowed his gaze at Seht. "Can we fuck now, '*Syr*?"

Seht grinned. "Certainly, pet." He gripped Aubrey around the thighs and sat up. Rising high up on his knees, he pulled Aubrey's butt up off the air mattress, leaving only his shoulders and head in contact.

Tipped nearly on his head, Aubrey yelped and threw out his arms, grabbing for the mattress.

Gripping Aubrey by the thighs, Seht pumped hard and fast into Aubrey's ass.

A wave of raw carnal ecstasy blazed up Aubrey's spine, raising the hair on his body. He arched and shouted. "Fuck!"

"Yes . . ." Seht licked his lips and ground into him, riding specifically on that hot swollen point within. "Cum, now!"

The vicious bolt of agonizing pleasure slammed up Aubrey's spine so fast, his body bowed hard and a shout was torn from his throat. Cum spilled, spattering down his chest, thick drops striking his cheeks.

He collapsed trembling and panting for breath.

"Excellent." Seht let him down on top the mattress, his cock easing free of Aubrey's butt. "It appears that I have mastered more of you than I thought."

Aubrey was too wrung out to even consider what Seht was saying. "Bleeding Fate, I don't think I've ever cum that fast."

Seht lifted his leg to straddle Aubrey's left thigh. "You are *rehkyt*." He pushed Aubrey's right leg over his knee, turning Aubrey's hips to the side.

Aubrey let Seht move him however he wanted. "What?"

Dovetailed between Aubrey's thighs, Seht leaned over Aubrey's body and stroked his tongue over Aubrey's erect and highly sensitive nipple. "Ready for more?"

A bolt of pleasure sizzled from Aubrey's nipple straight down to his dick. He shuddered and groaned. "More?"

"Absolutely." Seht leaned up, positioned his still rigid cock on Aubrey's anus, and pushed.

Aubrey felt Seht's cock slide into him with very little resistance. He groaned and hooked his bent knee around Seht's back without even thinking. "You're wearing my ass out, '*Syr*." The word just popped out of his mouth. He was too exhausted to even flinch.

Seht smiled. "That is my intent, pet." He leaned down on top of Aubrey's body, gripping his shoulders and pinning them to the mattress. He bowed his head and attacked Aubrey's nipple with his tongue.

White-hot bolts of pleasure spilled downward into Aubrey's dick, making it twitch, then fill. He grabbed Seht's upper arms, but there wasn't a drop of strength in his hands. "I can't . . ."

"You can." Seht bit down on the nipple and gently tugged with his teeth, then sucked.

Aubrey gasped out soft sounds of protest.

Seht merely switched nipples.

The sound of Aubrey's gasps changed until they sounded suspiciously close to whimpers.

Seht reached down with one hand and closed his fingers firmly around Aubrey's over-sensitive, and violently erect cock.

The sensation was ferocious and immediate. Aubrey couldn't stop his outcry. He grabbed for Seht's wrist with both hands.

Seht stilled and turned his blue gaze on Aubrey. A low growl rumbled in his chest. "Release me, pet."

Aubrey froze. His fingers loosened all by themselves. He eased his hands back and his chin lifted a little. He knew he was baring his throat, but he couldn't seem to stop himself.

Seht smiled, and it was pure evil. "Very good." He leaned up to press a light kiss on Aubrey's lips.

Hungry for reassurance, Aubrey opened his mouth.

Seht's tongue swept in to stroke against Aubrey's, then he slanted his mouth to take full hungry possession. His hand stroked down Aubrey's cock then upwards.

Aubrey jerked, his hips bucking in reflex. His moan was muffled by Seht's mouth. Needing something to hold on to, he grabbed Seht's shoulders.

With slow deliberation, Seht ground into Aubrey's body while stroking Aubrey's cock.

Unable to stop himself, Aubrey rocked against Seht's slow thrusts. Climax rose unbelievably fast to clench tight and knot in his balls. Small sounds of mounting distress poured from his throat.

Seht released Aubrey's lips and smiled. "Cum."

Climax erupted and burned like acid through him. He screamed. A thin stream of cum spilled across Seht's pumping hand and his body shuddered violently.

Seht smiled. "Good. You are very nearly empty." He leaned down and casually sank his teeth into Aubrey's shoulder. He licked the wounds. "Again."

Aubrey had barely had the presence of mind to realize that Seht had bitten him, but he knew damned well that his burning cock was getting hard again in Seht's cool stroking palm. "No! Please . . ." He knew he was begging and couldn't care less. His dick *hurt!*

Seht's lips brushed his ear. "Aubrey, to whom did you yield?" His hand continued to stroke.

Aubrey moaned and writhed. "You, *'Syr.'*" The answer left his lips completely without thought.

Seht ground into him and the fat knob of his knot at the base of his cock slid into Aubrey's ass. "And whom do you serve?"

Aubrey twisted under Seht and felt the knot swelling within him painfully tight. "You, *'Syr.'*"

Seht stroked his tongue up Aubrey's throat. "And how will you serve me?"

This time he knew the answer. He wanted to resist, but his body was too drained to summon up the energy. Tears spilled down Aubrey's cheeks. "With obedience, *'Syr.'*"

"Good pet." Seht gripped Aubrey's hair, arching his throat back. He slammed hard into Aubrey's body, then again, and again, grunting with each impact.

Aubrey cried out and bucked against him, unable to resist his body's reflexive reactions.

"Yes . . ." Seht groaned and ground deep into Aubrey. "Cum."

Aubrey stiffened. Climax exploded through Aubrey in a white-hot firestorm that broke his voice and burned his mind utterly blank.

Something warm and damp was sliding across his belly and thighs. It felt good. It felt comforting. It felt like . . . cloth? He could smell soap. Aubrey opened his eyes. His vision swam just a bit. His body was so utterly drained it actually took him several moments to focus, and a few more to gather the energy to turn his head.

Seht, naked, clean, and gleaming in the fire's light, leaned over him rubbing a cloth down his thighs, apparently washing him. His long mane was combed back into a snug braid that fell down his pale back.

Seht turned and smiled. "Ah, awake?" He sat back on his heels and wiped the back of his hand across his brow. "We were quite a bit of a mess, you and I."

Aubrey opened his mouth to say something but couldn't hold two thoughts together long enough to actually find something to say.

Seht reached out and ran his fingers through the hair falling across Aubrey's brow. "Ah . . . Your pupils are quite dilated. Feeling relaxed?"

Aubrey still couldn't find a word to say. He barely had the energy to lean into Seht's hand.

Seht slid his fingers down and pressed his palm to Aubrey's cheek. "Finally rendered speechless?"

Aubrey could care less what Seht was saying. All that really mattered was that Seht was touching him and smiling. He smiled back.

Seht snorted. "It seems so. Good, very good." He released Aubrey's cheek and turned away, reaching for something. "Only one more matter to attend to before we leave." He turned back with the smooth black box in his hand, the one that held the syringe. He opened it and carefully extracted a thin band of plain metal. Superfine electronic pins clustered inside one end.

Aubrey focused on the ring. A chill sweat broke out all over him.

Seht lifted his chin and focused on the cave's entrance. "It is still raining somewhat. Probably for the best." He looped the ring over his arm and leaned over Aubrey. "Come on, pet, we need to go outside the cave for this."

CHAPTER ELEVEN

With Seht's help, Aubrey was able to sit upright, but actually getting up and standing on his trembling legs was nearly impossible. Almost as soon as he was up on his feet, his knees buckled. He was just too exhausted.

Seht caught him around the chest and chuckled. "I have you." He half carried, half dragged Aubrey across the fine sand to the cave entrance, then into the chill darkness outside.

Ice cold drizzle spattered Aubrey's bare skin. He shivered.

Seht turned Aubrey to face the rain-damp cliff wall. "Go ahead and kneel, pet."

Aubrey didn't care that the ground was muddy, he collapsed to his knees gratefully.

Seht knelt behind him. "You're not going to like this, which is why I waited until I had you completely exhausted." He lowered the ring before Aubrey's gaze then closed it around his throat.

Aubrey stiffened, his entire body sizzling with alarm. *A collar. A damned collar!* He leaned away. "No." It came out as a whisper.

"I'm sorry, but this is how it must be." Seht reached around to press his palm against Aubrey's brow, holding his head up and still. "You have something embedded just at your hairline. No matter . . ." With one hard jab, he pressed the pins into the base of Aubrey's neck.

The pain was swift and sharp. Aubrey took in a deep breath. It was nothing compared to the airlock, but it had cleared some of the fog from his brain. A sudden sweat broke out all over his body. He frowned. *What the . . .*

A blinding power surge went through his internal array. He gasped. His entire body shuddered hard under the assault. From far away, he felt Seht grab his shoulders to keep him from knocking into the cliff face.

The surge spread down his spine. His fingers and toes twitched and his skin tried to crawl from his bones. He bit his lip to keep from howling. A moan escaped instead.

It stopped.

Soaked in sweat Aubrey panted, barely keeping himself upright on his knees.

Seht shifted behind him and took Aubrey's wrists, pulling his hands behind his back. "Just a bit more, pet." He set his palm back across Aubrey's forehead and barked out something in a language Aubrey didn't know.

Lightning blazed through him. He screamed and fought. Seht's grip was all that kept him from thrashing against the cliff wall.

The lightning stopped.

Aubrey moaned and tears streamed from his eyes. "Son of a bitch . . . What the hell was that?"

Seht released Aubrey's head and stroked his palm down Aubrey's shoulder. "That was the command setting for punishment."

Aubrey shuddered. "It's a fucking control collar."

"We call it a *shen*." Seht closed his arm around Aubrey's chest, embracing him, but didn't release his wrists. "*Rehkyt* are very aggressive by nature and can be very dangerous to anyone other than their master."

Aubrey stilled. "Dangerous? How dangerous?"

"Extremely." Seht pressed a kiss to the side of his brow. "Pushed too far, *Rehkyt* have been known to rape to relieve their urges, and then there is *rahyt*, blood-rage. A life threat to themselves or their masters can trigger a mindless killing rage in the more aggressive *rehkyt*." He snorted. "And you, my dear pet, are very aggressive indeed. The *shen* is designed specifically to stop a *rehkyt* that has gone beyond sense."

Aubrey could see the practicality, he really could, but wearing one still made his skin crawl. "Is that all it does?"

Seht sighed. "The *shen* is also a telepathic tracking device."

Aubrey turned his head away, his heart sinking in his chest. "I figured . . ."

Seht tightened his embrace. "Through the telepathic link, the *shen* allows you to find me as well."

Aubrey frowned. That was different. He hadn't heard of collars that worked both ways.

Seht's hands tightened around Aubrey's wrists. "This is the other command."

Aubrey stiffened. "Another one?"

Seht barked out another phrase.

Heat and lust burst in his belly, then clenched tight with hideous strength. All thought fled but for the heat in his cock. He writhed, moaning in urgent need.

Abruptly the vicious hunger relaxed its grip.

Aubrey gasped and shifted restlessly. The urgency was over, but his dick was violently hard.

Seht released his head and wrists.

Aubrey groaned and leaned against the cliff wall. "Bleeding Fate, I didn't think I could get hard again."

Behind him, Seht stood and brushed off his knees. "You are no longer human. Your body is capable of enduring a great deal."

"Fine, great, whatever . . ." Aubrey took in several deep breaths. "Are we done yet?"

"The telepathic commands are programmed. Turn around, and up on your knees."

Aubrey turned around to face Seht. It was an effort to rise up on his knees. He was forced to grab onto Seht's hips to keep from falling over. Despite his erection, he was still exhausted.

Seht stepped close, with his feet to either side of Aubrey's knees. He cupped his hand under Aubrey's chin. "Keep your head up."

Aubrey frowned up at him. "What . . ."

"Be still." Seht winced and groaned.

Hot liquid sprayed across Aubrey's belly, soaking his erection and thighs. The scent of urine burned his nose. Aubrey stiffened. Seht was pissing on him? Abruptly Aubrey's bladder reacted. Painfully fast, his erection left him. He closed his arms around Seht's waist and pressed his nose into Seht's belly. His control released, and his bladder emptied, all over Seht's feet.

Seht stiffened. "You did not . . ."

His face pressed against Seht's smooth belly Aubrey let a chuckle escape. "What? You did it to me."

Seht grabbed a handful of Aubrey's hair and jerked his head back. "I marked you for a reason, *rehkyt!*"

"Ow!" Aubrey winced. "Seht, what . . .?"

Seht grabbed Aubrey by the shoulders and pulled him up onto his feet. His nails dug bleeding furrows in Aubrey's skin. He slammed Aubrey against the cliff and pressed his body hard against Aubrey.

The wind woofed out of Aubrey's lungs. He gasped. "Ow! Shit . . ."

His eyes narrowed to feline slits, Seht bared his teeth in Aubrey's face and snarled. "Who is your master right here, right now, *rehkyt?*"

Aubrey couldn't stop staring at Seht's bared fangs. His heart slammed in his chest. Seht was seriously pissed off. But . . . But, he didn't want that. He didn't want Seht to be angry with him.

Huh? He stilled utterly. He didn't want Seht to be angry

with him? *What in bleeding Fate* . . . The hair on his body rose. He'd had hoped that Seht hadn't really meant what he'd said about mastering his mind as well as his body, but this strange need to please said otherwise.

Seht dug his nails in viciously and pulled Aubrey from the cliff face, then slammed him back against it again. "Answer me, damn you! Who is your master?"

The stone bruised his naked back. Aubrey gasped. "You, 'Syr."

Seht curled his fingers through the front of Aubrey's collar and tugged him close, practically nose to nose. His angry feline gaze speared into Aubrey and his liquid growl rumbled. "I claim you by right of conquest as mine; my property, my pet, and my slave. Do you yield to my claim?"

Aubrey shivered with more than just the chill of the rain. "Yes, 'Syr." Shock and despair warred in his heart. The answer had come far too easily. But what shook him to the core, was that some small place at the bottom of his heart was pleased to say it.

"At last . . ." Seht pressed Aubrey up against the cliff-side and took his mouth in a brutal kiss that left no question as to who was master.

Aubrey couldn't stop from clinging to Seht's shoulders, and his kiss, any more than he could stop the rain or the tears.

Aubrey snapped awake on his side under the blanket. Seht was warm against his back with his arm flung over Aubrey's hip. He frowned. The last thing he remembered was being outside in the rain. He shifted and winced. The hot length of Seht's cock was wedged deep in his ass, again.

Seht sighed against the back of his neck and his hand slid along Aubrey's belly in a light caress.

Aubrey shivered and felt a warm sleepy curl of heat spill downward. His cock pulsed and swelled with rising heat.

Warm waves of erotic excitement mixed with twinges from his tender abdominal muscles. He sucked in a breath. *What in hell . . .* His whole body ached, and his ass hurt like hell, but here he was, getting excited yet again.

Seht's long nails dug into his flanks lightly and a rumbling growl vibrated against Aubrey's back.

Aubrey's whole body clenched in sudden and voracious anticipation.

Damn it! What was it with his body? He'd never had a problem handling pain. All the beatings in the world hadn't made a dent on him. But his libido was like a starving beast just begging to be fucked. He bit down on his lip, straining to calm himself. This had to stop. He had to gain control of his himself before he became little more than a raging nympho-maniac. He did not want to be reduced to little more than a fuck-toy.

Seht chuckled and pressed a kiss to his shoulder. "And what, pray tell, is so terrible about being a nymphomaniac?"

Aubrey jumped. "How did . . ."

Seht tapped a long nail against Aubrey's collar. "Telepathic link."

Aubrey stilled and an icy sweat spread across his back. "You're in my head?" Like Niobe, and that insane nav-pilot?

Seht snorted. "No, not like those. I am not *in* your mind. I can feel some of your emotions and hear any clear thoughts you project. That is all."

Aubrey cringed. "It's still creepy."

Seht chuckled. "You will become accustomed, over time."

"Great . . ." Aubrey rubbed the raised hair on his arms. "I can hardly wait."

"And you are *not* a mere fuck-toy." Seht's arms tightened around him. "Your mind is too valuable to waste. I intend to have you properly trained."

"Trained?" Aubrey curled his lip. "As what?"

"My personal pilot, at the very least."

Aubrey blinked. "Oh . . ." That didn't sound so bad. "I'm good with ships." Really good, in fact, too good. That was how he'd ended up with a penal tracker in the back of his neck, and Moribund hunting him.

Seht chuckled. "You will make an excellent pilot; in addition to being my personal fuck-toy." He swept a wet tongue along the ridge of Aubrey's spine.

"Ah! Seht . . ." Aubrey shivered and squirmed. *Crap, not more sex!* "I can't . . . do any more!" He twisted to look back at Seht. "Seriously, I can't!"

Seht smiled. "Yes, yes, I know." He slid a hand up Aubrey's ribs. "You are severely undernourished and your body is still processing. You have yet to reach your full strength." He slid his fingers into Aubrey's overgrown hair and watched the strands slip through. "I simply enjoy touching you." His brow lifted and his gaze focused. "You should go back to sleep. We leave for my ship at sunset."

Aubrey groaned. "I don't know if I *can* sleep." He was dead tired sure, but his thoughts were a snarled mess from all that had happened since he'd been pulled from the tank.

"Aubrey . . ." Seht caught Aubrey's chin and stared hard into his eyes. "Sleep. Now."

Blackness crashed over Aubrey's mind.

CHAPTER TWELVE

Aubrey tugged on his ship-suit watching Seht shove everything back into his backpack. He zipped the suit closed. The baggy thing seemed to fit better. Had it shrunk in the rain? *Must be really cheap material.* He turned to look over at Seht and frowned. "Seht, did you *make* me sleep?"

Seht turned around and shoved a squeeze bottle of protein drink into Aubrey's hand. "Yes."

Yes? Aubrey set the bottle beside him and pulled on his boots. Seht just told him to sleep, and he slept? He rose to his feet and swallowed a mouthful of the protein drink. He didn't know what to think about that.

Seht shouldered his pack and the bolt rifle. "We need to move quickly. I do not know if Moribund is still searching for you." He strode for the cave entrance.

Aubrey sighed and followed. "Hopefully, they think I dropped dead."

Seht flashed a fanged smile over his shoulder. "One can hope."

Aubrey stepped out among the tall rocks and stared up at a puke green and rancid orange sky. "At least it's not raining."

Seht looked at his wrist band. "Not at the moment, but we should hurry if we wish to arrive dry."

The march out of the ravine was steep but not particularly difficult. However, Aubrey's boots were pinching his toes. At first it was merely an annoyance, but the further they walked, the worse it got.

Seht stopped in the middle of the brush-lined path. "Take

off your boots."

Aubrey stopped and stared at Seht's back. "Huh?"

Seht turned around and scowled. "Your boots are hurting your feet. Take them off."

Aubrey frowned. *How* . . . Oh yeah, the damned telepathic collar. "You think going barefoot is going to be any easier?"

"For you, yes." Seht sighed. "Your feet will callus very quickly, you heal that fast. For the same reason, leaving your feet in those undersized boots could cause your bones to form improperly."

Aubrey frowned. "Cause my *bones* to form improperly?"

Seht rolled his eyes. "You are still developing under the influence of the injections. The nanites are still active in your body."

"Oh . . ." Aubrey sat on the path to pull off his boots.

Seht folded his arms. "Haven't you noticed? You have already gained in height."

Aubrey stilled. "I have?" He was taller? No, he hadn't noticed.

Seht snorted. "Quickly. I must get to my *barque* and return to the warship before Lord Syrhus sends out a search party." He looked back up the path. "If he has not already."

Aubrey tossed his boots into the bushes and rose to his feet. He wriggled his toes. They felt better already. "Who's this Lord Syrhus?"

Seht turned away and continued up the near invisible path. "Lord Syrhus is the captain of the warship, my cousin, and the husband of my exalted sister."

Aubrey frowned. His cousin had married his sister? "So that makes him, your . . . brother-in-law?" Or was he an uncle? Aubrey trotted after Seht. The ground wasn't exactly comfortable to walk on, but at least his toes weren't being pinched.

Seht sighed. "My sister is *Hedjhyt,* the crown princess and heir to the throne. Syrhus is her *Atehf*, prince consort." He looked back over his shoulder at Aubrey. "And someone you do not speak to or make eye contact with." He looked forward. "In fact, if you are addressed by any *Skeldhi*, it would be best if you did not speak at all, merely bow to acknowledge their attention; it's polite."

"Bow to be polite, I can do that . . ." Aubrey shook his head. "Wait a minute . . . Your sister is the crown princess? What does that make you?"

Seht shoved a bush out of his way. "It makes me *Deshryt*, a blood prince."

Aubrey tripped over nothing in particular. "You're a . . . *prince*?"

Seht shrugged. "It does not amount to much more than a small palace by the sea. The females rule our government and control commerce, so a male is only as good as the battles he can win, and the daughters he can produce."

Aubrey frowned. "That sounds kind of . . . crappy."

Seht chuckled. "It is not so bad." He adjusted the pack slung over his shoulders. "I am serving on my brother-in-law's warship in preparation to become captain of my own."

"Oh . . ." Aubrey puzzled over what else Seht had mentioned. "And I'm not supposed to talk to Lord Syrhus, or look him in the eye?"

"Do not look any *skeldhis* directly in the eye; they'll take it as a direct challenge. Do not show your teeth for exactly the same reason, even in a smile."

Aubrey snorted. "What if I *want* to challenge them?"

Seht turned sharply and snarled. "Do you want to end up in a muzzle?"

Aubrey jerked to a startled halt. "A . . . what?"

Seht's gaze narrowed. "*Rehkyt* that bite are kept bound and in muzzles, in the same fashion as a canine that bites."

A chill raised the small hairs on the back of Aubrey's neck.

"You're shitting me . . ."

Seht's jaw tightened. "No, I am not."

Crap! Aubrey swallowed. "Okay, all right . . . No biting."

Seht nodded. "Good." He turned and started up the path. "Hands above the waist are also a sign of aggression, so keep your hands below your waist, unless ordered to do otherwise. Your place is one step back and only on my left side, so as not to interfere with my sword-draw."

Aubrey frowned. "You wear a sword?"

Seht smiled briefly. "Normally, yes. I wished to travel light so most of my weapons, and my armor, are still in my *barque*."

Aubrey blinked. Swords and armor . . ."Will I get to use a sword?"

Seht shoved his way into a clump of spiny brush. "I can arrange for training . . . In fact, I probably should arrange for *upuaht*, guard training, though you might not like it."

Aubrey followed him into the bushes. "Why not?"

"*Rehkyt* training is done by *nehkyx*. The word means 'whip'. You would remain with them and be under their complete control until they decide you have mastered what they have to teach you. Normally that would be for several months, at the very least. Some training takes years to master."

Aubrey shrugged. "Sounds like any other school."

Seht turned and frowned at Aubrey. "Do you normally service your instructors?"

"Service . . ." Aubrey blinked. "You mean have sex with them?" A sour smile curled his lip. "From what I hear, it's not unusual for an academy instructor to bend a student over their desk."

Seht's brows lifted. "Is that so?"

Aubrey shook his head. "It's not something I ever had to deal with. I didn't go to the military academy." *Dad wasn't that rich.* He'd had 'public school' all the way.

"I see . . ." Seht pursed his lips. "If I turn you over to a *nehkyx*, sexual service is not only expected, it is required."

"Required?" Aubrey tripped. He'd *have to* have sex with somebody other than Seht? He could barely deal with having sex with Seht. He wasn't sure he could deal with anybody else. He swallowed. "Seriously?"

Seht shrugged. "A *rehkyt's* mental and physical health depends on regular sexual release. The *nehkyx* is expected to handle those needs in place of the absent master."

Aubrey groaned. "Oh, come on, I can always just jerk-off."

Seht snorted. "Not anymore. Your body will no longer achieve orgasm that way."

Aubrey froze in mid-step. "Say . . . what?" He stared at Seht.

Seht shrugged. "You are *rehkyt*. You need more stimuli to achieve orgasm than . . . that."

Aubrey frowned. That sounded like a load of crap if ever he'd heard one. "So what kind of . . . stimuli are we talking about here?"

Seht smiled, showing fangs. "I will take great pleasure in showing you."

Aubrey snorted. "Now you're just teasing me."

"Which reminds me . . ." Seht held up a finger. "No one touches you without my express permission. Not even Lord Syrhus." He turned to look at Aubrey. "You are mine, and mine alone."

Aubrey lifted a brow. "Okay . . ." Was he supposed to be happy or scared?

Seht shoved further into the brush. "This means that if you prove troublesome to others, I will bear the brunt of your disgrace." He turned and shot a narrow look at Aubrey. "After which, I will take my ire out on your skin."

Aubrey couldn't help but smile. "What are you going to do, beat me?"

"Yes." Seht smiled right back, showing his complete set of

fangs. "I did not wear my whip as I did not have a personal *rehkyt*, but I will be sure to introduce you to it at our first convenient moment."

Aubrey's smile evaporated. "What, are you actually looking forward to beating me?"

Seht's evil smile widened. "I am quite sure that you will look spectacular dancing under my whip." He frowned. "As soon as you gain a bit more muscle."

"Uh . . ." The hair on Aubrey's neck rose, and yet a small curl of heat spilled downward. He frowned. If he didn't know better, he'd think his body wanted to be whipped.

Seht chuckled and moved up the path. "I assure you, you will enjoy it."

Aubrey jerked back. "Enjoy what? Being whipped?"

Seht slid between two tall rocks. "*Rehkyt* are designed to need extreme stimulus as much as they need sex."

Aubrey followed after him frowning. Extreme stimulus and sex? "You're saying I'm designed to be . . . kinky?"

"Yes." Seht turned sharply to scowl at Aubrey. "And obedient."

Aubrey jerked to an abrupt halt. "Yes, '*Syr!*'" He froze, shocked. That had come out of his mouth purely by reflex. *Crap . . . He's deeper in my head than I thought.*

Seht smiled sweetly and reached out to pat Aubrey on the head. "Good pet."

Aubrey scowled and glared at Seht's back. *Fine, rub it in.*

Two steps ahead of him, Seht chuckled.

Aubrey plucked a leaf from a nearby bush. "So . . . What I'm supposed to do, as your pet?" He tossed the leaf and scowled after it.

Seht shoved a branch out of his way. "What is expected of you is very much like any pet you might have had."

"Oh, really?" Aubrey snorted and followed him. "Does this mean I have to stay off the furniture?"

"Yes." Seht didn't even look back.

Aubrey choked. "That was a joke!"

"Actually, it is not. You are to kneel by my feet when I am seated."

What the hell . . . Heat flashed at the back of Aubrey's skull. He winced and rubbed just at his hairline. His fingers brushed the collar. *Collars, muzzles, no sitting on the furniture . . .* Just how far did the Skeldhi take this human pet . . . thing? "Do I have to wear a leash too?"

"On occasion." Seht didn't even look back.

Aubrey's mind went utterly blank for three whole breaths. "Seht, I'm not an animal."

Seht continued to walk. "You are no longer human."

Aubrey trotted to catch up to him. "I know that, but I'm not some dangerous insane beast either!"

Seht shook his head. "That remains to be seen."

Aubrey curled his lip. "Give it a freaking break . . ."

Seht laughed and lengthened his stride. "You are most definitely feeling better."

Aubrey followed Seht out of the ravine at full dark. At least, Aubrey was pretty sure it was full dark. He could see the occasional star twinkling between clouds and there wasn't a trace of sunlight. However, it didn't seem exactly . . . dark. He had no problems seeing anything, even in deep shadow.

Seht lifted his head and looked about. His snowy hair practically glowed. "It seems clear, but we should proceed with caution." He pointed. "My *barque* is at the base of that rock formation."

Aubrey frowned at the tall jagged rocks Seht seemed to be indicating. He saw stunted trees and some low shrubs, but that was all. "I don't see a ship."

Seht leaned close. "If you look carefully, you'll notice that the air seems . . . heavier just at the base of the tallest stone?"

Aubrey frowned. The air did seem to be wavering a little.

"It just looks like rising heat."

Seht nodded. "The *barque* is currently reflecting its surroundings as camouflage."

Aubrey's brows lifted. "That's an interesting trick." He'd never seen a ship blend in with its surroundings so well. "What is it mimetic or something?"

"Yes, that also." Seht eased down into the thinner scrub. "Keep your voice down."

Aubrey frowned and mentally thumbed through his internal files. Mimetic objects shape-changed, some on only a small scale such as a live-steel sword that would always retain its edge, but some ships were capable of making themselves actually seamless and mirror smooth. He moved to Seht's left side and pitched his voice to a low whisper. "You're saying the ship's entire hull is nano-enhanced?"

"Actually, the entire ship is mimetic, inside and out." Seht smiled, flashing a long tooth. "Extremely difficult to steal."

Aubrey pursed his lips. "I could see how that would pose a problem to joy-riders." To get onboard, he'd literally have to negotiate with the ship's artificial intelligence. He was pretty sure he had a subroutine that might work . . .

Seht frowned at him.

Aubrey wiped his thoughts from his mind and pasted on the most innocent smile he could summon while carefully concealing his teeth. "What?"

Seht shook his head and sighed. "You are clearly going to be a handful."

Aubrey snorted. "Wouldn't want you to get bored."

Seht shot a narrowed look Aubrey's way. "You definitely need a beating."

Aubrey smiled. "You know, my dad used to say that a lot . . ." The scent of . . . musty sweaty cloth caught Aubrey's attention. It smelled familiar. It smelled like . . . his ship-suit. He frowned. "Why do I smell . . ."

Seht jerked to a halt and lifted his nose. "Damn!" He turned and dove at Aubrey, arms wide.

Aubrey didn't have a chance to react. He was slammed onto the ground, landing hard on his back with Seht on top of him. The air woofed out of his lungs. He gasped in a breath.

Seht shoved his hand over Aubrey's mouth. *Do not speak aloud.* He looked to the side, peering through the undergrowth and eased the bolt rifle from his shoulder. *It seems that Moribund has yet to give up on you.*

Aubrey's eyes opened wide. Seht's words were crystal clear in his head, but he knew for a fact he hadn't actually heard a thing. *Telepathy?*

Of course. Seht glanced at Aubrey. *You have a good nose.* He smiled. *You caught scent of them before I did.*

Rocks scattered loudly. "What?" The voice was breathy, masculine, and sounded close.

Aubrey turned to look through the brush but didn't see anything.

"I thought I saw something." The other voice was just as breathy, as though they were attempting to whisper.

About four body-lengths away, the brush moved. A man wearing foot-soldier battle armor stepped out from behind the brush. The visor on his helmet glowed green, indicating that his night-sight was active. The green light gleamed along the long barrel of his bolt rifle. "That kid has to be dead by now. There is no way he could have survived this atmosphere this long."

A smaller man followed him from the scrub, also in armor and wearing a night-sighted helmet. He looked about. The barrel of his rifle pointed where Seht and Aubrey lay concealed, then passed. "So we're looking for a body, right?"

Aubrey frowned. Their voices sounded a hell of a lot closer than they actually were.

"A dark-haired and scrawny body." The first guy moved further into the open. "So if it's moving and has white hair, shoot it."

"A body, huh?" The smaller man turned back on his companion and began walking backwards, clearly covering for his partner. "And what are we supposed to do with this body, carry it all the way back?"

The first guy turned and held up a black bag. "We only need the head, stupid."

"And if the kid is still alive?"

The larger man shrugged and continued progressing through the brush, his boots making an incredible amount of crunching noises. "We bring the brat back with us."

The smaller man snorted. "It'd be easier to just bring the head back. Accidents can happen, you know."

The larger man shook his head. "I heard *he* plans to tap that brain. I don't know about you, but I really don't want that kid to have a memory of me shooting him." He nodded significantly. "Not when *he* prefers that kid alive." The two mercenaries stepped among the taller rocks and out of sight.

Aubrey clenched his jaw. *He* could only be Moribund. The man he had never seen; the man that had forced him to kill so many people. Heat seared the back of his skull. A memory flashed. A long shard of steel sinking into a uniformed body . . . Hot red liquid spilling over his hands . . . The smell of raw meat . . . Something in his chest vibrated and rumbled.

Seht looked down at him and raised a brow. *You're growling.*

Huh? Aubrey's thoughts stilled. He blinked up at Seht, shocked. *I'm . . . growling?*

Seht eased up off of Aubrey, rising into a squat. He slid his bolt rifle off his shoulder and into his hands. His fanged smile was chilling. *You were saying something about not being a beast?*

Shut up! That's when he realized that he was also baring his fangs. He sat up cautiously and felt his cheeks heat furiously. *Crap . . .*

Seht waved at Aubrey. *This way.* Moving quietly, they

strode across the clearing and downhill into deep brush.

CHAPTER THIRTEEN

Seht stopped cold among the standing stones at the edge of a broad clearing. *Damn . . .*

Only a step behind him, Aubrey stared at the wavering air that marked Seht's hidden ship just on the other side of the clearing.

Seht grabbed the front of Aubrey's suit and hauled Aubrey behind a large rock.

Held fast in Seht's grip, Aubrey teetered off balance. *What the . . .*

Seht dropped into a crouch, pulling Aubrey down with him. *We are not alone.*

A flurry of whizzing pops echoed between the tall rocks from more than one direction accompanied by shouts in several languages.

Aubrey sucked in a sharp breath. It sounded like a lot of men, with a lot of guns. Just how many people were hunting him?

Seht peeked past the edge of a jagged stone. *I do not think they have seen us.*

Aubrey knelt up and strained to look past Seht's shoulder. *Then, who are they shooting at?*

Stay down. Seht pushed Aubrey back. *From the voices, it appears that my cousin grew impatient and came for me.*

Oh . . . Aubrey scraped a hand through his hair. *So, how are we supposed to get past this?*

We go around it. Seht looked over at Aubrey. *Are you good for a fast run?*

Aubrey snorted. He wasn't even winded. He grinned. *Just try to leave me behind.*

Seht raised a brow at him. *You're showing teeth.*

Aubrey's grin dissolved into a scowl. *Well, excuse me for smiling.*

Seht rolled his eyes. *You can smile; just avoid baring your teeth while you do it.*

Aubrey had to work to suppress a growl. Of all the stupid things to bitch about . . . *Can we worry about that later, when people aren't shooting for us?*

Stubborn brat! Seht bared his teeth and released a low growl. *I am definitely beating you at my first opportunity.* He bolted back the way he they had come, zigzagging between the rocks.

Aubrey lunged after him. What in bleeding Fate was *his* problem?

The run through the rocks and brush was a howling mess of gunshots, violent shouts and moving shadows caused by flashes of too bright light from muzzle fire. And blood. The smell of wet copper and raw meat was overpowering. It was also arousing. He was getting hard, and hungry.

Aubrey nearly tripped. *What the hell . . .* What kind of freak got turned on from blood? Never mind that, how the hell was he supposed to run with a hard-on? His trousers tightened and his steps faltered. *Shit . . .* He grabbed himself to set his dick a bit more comfortably and nearly lost sight Seht in the process.

Seht stopped and looked back at Aubrey, frowning.

Aubrey hurried to catch up.

A red flower bloomed on Seht's left upper thigh and dripped. As though in slow motion, Seht's eyes widened and his lips parted. He turned sharply to the side, slamming back against a standing stone, and collapsed.

Shock blazed at the back of Aubrey's skull. *Seht!* He didn't think, he threw out his hands and leaped, putting every ounce of power into his legs. He landed practically on top of Seht, very nearly falling on him, and dragged him behind a rock.

Seht gasped on the ground. *No need to shout. It is merely a bolt.* He lifted a hand. *Move back.*

Merely a bolt, he says . . . Aubrey moved back and crouched down, unsure of what to do.

This is not my first bolt wound. Seht sat up and scowled, baring his teeth. He took a breath and grabbed the leg of his suit. *I doubt it will be my last.* He dug his long nails into the tear and ripped the fabric, exposing the bullet hole. *At least it is not in a vital area.* He grabbed at his sleeve and wrenched. The fabric ripped from the shoulder and came free.

Aubrey blinked. He couldn't have done that. He sighed. *Oh yeah . . .* Seht was mechanically augmented, where he wasn't.

A whisper of pain throbbed in Aubrey's leg. He winced. Apparently, words weren't the only things transferred through the telepathic link in the collar. Aubrey could also feel something else. Something freezing hot searing between his eyes and raising the hair on the back of his neck. Aubrey blinked. Anger, he was feeling anger. Seht was furious.

Idiots . . . Seht wrapped the sleeve around his left leg and a growl rumbled from him. *We would have made it.* He knotted the sleeve with sharp jerks. *But oh no, Syrhus just had to come down and stir this viper's nest!* He grabbed Aubrey's shoulder. *Help me up.*

Aubrey grabbed Seht under his arm and around his waist to lever Seht onto his feet and against Aubrey's right side. He groaned under Seht's weight. *Bloody Fate, you weigh a ton.*

Seht snorted. *Ah, yes . . .* He looped his arm around Aubrey's shoulders, balancing on his right leg. *You have no augmentations.*

And you do. Aubrey readjusted his grip to free his left hand. *Give me the rifle.*

Seht looped the rifle's strap over his shoulder so that the rifle draped on his right side out of Aubrey's reach. *No.*

Aubrey stared at him. *You can't shoot it . . .*

Forget the rifle! Seht leaned forward, forcing Aubrey to step forward or fall over. *Go!*

Aubrey went. Side by side, they limped forward at a fairly swift walk with Aubrey acting as Seht's crutch. Aubrey's feeling of discomfort grew stronger. He didn't like being unarmed with Seht wounded. If they were attacked, there wasn't a damned thing he could do about it. *Can I have a knife at least?*

Seht sighed heavily. *Very well . . .* He pulled his long dagger and sheath from his belt at the small of his back. *Do not pull it unless there is need, and for Night's sake, do not pull it before any skeldhis!*

Yeah, fine, whatever . . . Aubrey took the sheathed dagger. He jammed it into the slender belt around his suit and felt a hell of a lot better. *I just don't like being unarmed.*

Seht snorted. *Apparently not. You have been grumbling about it for a while.*

Aubrey winced. He was going to have to do something about guarding his thoughts.

They turned past a group of boulders and Aubrey froze. Every hair on his body rose, and an icy sweat formed down his back. Something wasn't right.

Seht frowned at him. *What is it?*

Aubrey stepped back, urging Seht back the way they'd come. *I don't know.* He wasn't sure what was wrong, but something definitely wasn't right. He looked around sharply. He didn't see anything or hear anything other than the wind . . . He sucked in a sharp breath. That was it; the silence. The shooting and shouting had stopped.

Seht's fingers on his shoulder dug in. *Over there.* He raised his chin toward the right.

Aubrey pulled Seht back and shoved him back against a stone, then pulled his hands free of Seht.

Seht winced and teetered off balance. He grabbed the stone

for balance. *Aubrey* . . .

His heart pounding in his mouth, Aubrey turned his back to Seht, pressing him back against the stone.

Seht gasped. *Aubrey!*

Aubrey pulled the long knife from the sheath.

Four fully armored men stepped from the surrounding rocks. They froze.

One of the armored men tilted his helmeted head. "Holy fuck, the kid is still alive!"

The one in the center wearing officer's bars raised his hand. "Take it easy, kid, we've come here to get you."

Aubrey held up the knife. "Go the fuck away."

"Who's that behind him?"

Seht swung the rifle forward, the long barrel pointing past Aubrey. "Good evening, gentlemen. If you'll excuse us, my pet and I are on our way home."

The officer nodded. "Somebody shoot that."

Aubrey held out his arms, bared his long teeth and growled. "Nobody touches him."

"Don't shoot the kid!"

"Hey, is he supposed to have fangs? I thought he was human?"

"Ah, fuck . . . He's been bit."

"Who gives a shit, as long as he's still breathing?"

"Yeah, but now we know why he's breathing."

Aubrey had no clue what they were talking about and didn't particularly care. He could barely think past the white burning at the back of his skull. It wasn't fear, it was anticipation. If they took one step closer, he was going to rip their hearts out. His lips curled into a fanged smile.

Seht chuckled. "Gentlemen, I really think you should let us pass before it is too late."

The officer waved. "Ignore that and get the kid."

Two men shouldered their rifles and moved toward

Aubrey. Seht's rifle went off very close to Aubrey's head. Sound disappeared completely and one man fell.

Aubrey tightly focused on the man left and lunged. The world drifted into slow motion. It was a simple matter to duck, avoiding the hands reaching for him and dip his knife into the unprotected arm joint of the man's armor. As though he had all the time in the world, he carefully angled for the heart. He pushed deep and twisted. He stepped back, pulling the knife free at the same time. Scarlet sprayed in a slow, lovely arc.

It felt right. It felt good. No, it felt better than good, it felt great! He grinned.

The man folded at his feet.

He raced for the man standing nearby. Dodging the grasping hands was so very easy. So was stabbing upward under the jaw of the helmet. He pulled his knife free and twisted away from the spray of liquid rubies.

Hunger burned in his belly. He raised his knife and licked at the warm blood running down the steel. It wasn't enough. He wanted meat. He focused on the last enemy before him. The heart . . . He was willing to bet he could rip it out and bite into it before it stopped beating.

Somewhere at the back of his mind, someone was shouting his name. He ignored it.

The enemy trembled, and the bitter perfume of fear filled the air between them. The man dropped where he stood.

Disappointment crashed down. A howl ripped from his throat. Sound abruptly returned.

"Aubrey!"

He stiffened. That voice . . . He knew that voice. He turned.

Leaning heavily against a tall rock was a beautiful silver-haired boy. A rifle was slung over his shoulder in an unthreatening manner. The scent of sweat and blood rolled from his body. It was a familiar aroma. It was a delicious aroma. The boy held out his hand. "Come, pet. Come to me." His voice was gentle but firm.

A chill raced from the back of his skull straight down his spine, leaving shivers in its wake. His hands shook. He took a step toward the boy on shaking legs, and then another. The knife fell from nerveless fingers.

Tall pale shadows glided at the edges of his vision.

The boy's gaze darted from side to side, then focused on him. "Look at me, pet, only at me."

He stepped closer, drawn by the voice, and the perfume of his skin. Thought surfaced through the burning haze in his mind. He blinked. "Seht?" His knees wobbled and he reached out toward him.

"Yes." Seht kept his hand out, and a crooked smile bloomed. "I can't go to you. You have to come to me."

Aubrey's gaze was drawn to the rag tied around his leg. *That's right, he was shot.* He lurched to Seht and grabbed for his hand. His knees gave out and he collapsed in a trembling heap at Seht's feet. He wanted nothing more than to pass out right there.

"Very good." Seht slid his fingers through Aubrey's tangled hair. "How do you feel?"

Aubrey snorted and then groaned. "Like total crap."

Seht frowned at him, his gaze darting about. "Are you wounded?"

Aubrey lifted his arms to look at them, then tugged at his ship-suit. Blood was spattered everywhere, and several rents had been torn into his suit, but the sting of cut flesh seemed to be missing. "Doesn't feel like it."

Seht released a soft breath and flashed a small smile. "Good."

Half a dozen tall, dark shadows eased from behind rocks and brush to become men in decorative black helmets and armor, bearing swords, and bolt rifles.

Aubrey stiffened.

It's all right. Seht continued to stroke Aubrey's hair. *Just stay as you are.*

A man in a deep green cape, his shoulders enveloped in black fur stepped forward. He pulled the black helmet from his head releasing a cascade of white hair. Thousands of green beads gleamed among the tiny braids of his hair. An iridescent black circlet graced his brow above gleaming blue eyes that held the deep green glow of reflected light. "*Deshryt* Seht." He crossed his arms and frowned deeply. "You are late."

Aubrey blinked. *Eh?*

"*Atehf* Syrhus." Seht dropped his gaze and delivered a short bow. "You could have left me. My ship is jump capable."

Aubrey's brows rose. *This* was Seht's uncle? Cousin? Both?

Syrhus's gaze shifted to Aubrey and his brows lifted.

Aubrey pulled his gaze away just in time to avoid a direct stare. He didn't want this man focusing on him, though he wasn't sure why.

Syrhus shifted his gaze back to Seht and scowled. "As long as you are in my care, you will be accounted for at all times."

Seht snorted. "I am so blessed, '*Syr.*'" Sarcasm dripped from his words.

Aubrey tilted his head. *He called him 'Syr?* Apparently, that word was a standard form of address to one's superior. Suddenly his resistance to the word felt a little . . . silly.

"And you will count those blessings once we reach the ship, I promise you." Syrhus nodded toward Aubrey. "Would you care to explain *that?*"

Seht lifted his chin. "*That* is mine."

Syrhus sighed and scraped a hand through his long, beaded mane. "In the midst of a raid . . ." He curled his lip, revealing one long fang. "Only you would stop to pick up a half-starving stray."

Stray? Aubrey felt a growl begin to rise. He took a very deep breath to smother it.

Seht's fingers bit hard into Aubrey's shoulder. Apparently, he wasn't happy with Syrhus's words either.

Syrhus's gaze narrowed and focused, staring hard at Aubrey. He frowned. "Please tell me that *that* is not the prey Moribund was stalking?"

Aubrey turned sharply away and glared at the ground.

Seht's nails dug into Aubrey's shoulder. "It is, *'Syr.'*"

Syrhus sighed and wiped a hand down his face. "How many doses?"

Seht's expression shifted to something like mild disinterest. "On his second, *'Syr.'*"

Abruptly, Syrhus turned away to face the other pale shadows and snapped out something in a language Aubrey couldn't begin to decipher.

Aubrey looked up at Seht. *Is there a problem?*

Seht stroked his shoulder, but anger shimmered at the back of his thoughts. *No.*

Syrhus turned back to Seht. "Come."

Seht stiffened. "My *barque* . . ."

"You are going to it. However, you're in no condition to pilot anything." Syrhus stared pointedly at the blood sliding down his leg.

Seht bowed briefly. "Yes, *'Syr.'*"

Syrhus turned and started walking.

Seht patted Aubrey's shoulder. *Time to go home.*

Aubrey rose, or rather, he tried to. His legs utterly refused to cooperate. Panic slammed into his heart. He looked up at Seht in alarm and watched the boy's pale face disappear down a long dark tunnel.

CHAPTER FOURTEEN

Aubrey opened his eyes to a low domed ceiling lit by small dim lights along the curved wall, and the softness of a mattress under him. The bed and the room around it appeared to be round. An echo of pain radiated in his heart. *Another needle?*

Yes. Seht eased down onto his knees and leaned over Aubrey with a soft smile. His silver mane spilled down one shoulder to drape across Aubrey's bare chest. He swept his hand through Aubrey's overlong red hair and a wave of affection pulsed straight from Seht's mind to his. *How do you feel?*

Aubrey blinked. How *did* he feel? For some reason, it was hard to tell. He went to lift his hand and found it ridiculously hard to do. He frowned briefly and persevered until he was able to touch Seht's hand. *I think I'm okay, just tired.* He spotted a white patch behind the rent in the upper thigh of Seht's shipsuit. *How about you?*

Seht snorted. *I'll be fully recovered by the time we reach home, as will you.* He grinned. *I have so much to show you.*

Aubrey looked around, but there wasn't anything to see. They appeared to be sitting in a very small oval room that consisted of silvery oval walls, a mattress, and nothing else. "Where . . ." His voice came out very hoarse and it was surprisingly painful. He winced and coughed. *Ow . . .*

Seht pressed his fingers over Aubrey's lips. *Don't try to talk. You've damaged your vocal cords.*

Aubrey blinked up at him. *I have?*

Seht snorted. *Apparently, you like to scream when you fight.*

Aubrey rolled his eyes. *Oh.* He frowned. *I thought I was supposed to heal fast?*

Seht nodded. *You do and you are. However, your entire body is currently undergoing cellular reconstruction, plus you're malnourished. This will slow the healing process somewhat.*

A hole appeared in the wall behind Seht, and Syrhus leaned in. "Is it finished?"

Seht sighed. "I've administered the third dose and given him a full battery of vitamin boosters." He reached up and a tube formed from the curve of the ceiling, then dangled down. Seht lifted a cuff from his side and attached the tube to it. "I'm setting up the protein drip to feed him." He looped the cuff around Aubrey's wrist. "This should hold him until we can get him properly fed."

Aubrey felt the tiny pins stabbing into his wrist, then the slight chill from the liquid feeding directly into his veins.

Syrhus nodded. "Good." He waved a hand indicating that Seht should leave. "Come."

Seht looked back toward Aubrey. "I just dosed him, I haven't . . ."

Aubrey's face heated. He knew exactly what Seht was talking about; they hadn't had sex yet.

Syrhus shook his head. "There is time for that yet. You have a report to deliver. Now."

Seht scowled but backed out of the tiny room. "Yes, *Syr*." He patted Aubrey's hand and delivered a small smile. *I'll be back soon.* He stepped back and the opening in the wall spiraled closed.

Aubrey settled back among the cushions and closed his eyes in an attempt to take a nap. Unfortunately, his body had other ideas, namely, his bladder. He scowled. Damn it. He sat up and pulled off the cuff around his wrist.

Something beeped.

Seht's alarmed presence was suddenly loud and clear in his

mind. *Aubrey, is something wrong?*

Aubrey winced while his face warmed with embarrassment. *I need to . . . pee.*

Humor skittered across their link, but along with it came a sudden daydream-like vision showing a pale hand pressing against the wall to open the door to his little room, then the ship's narrow hall. Two doors down on the right was the tiny facility.

Aubrey didn't hesitate. He slapped his palm on the wall to make it spiral open and dashed out into the silver-walled hallway on legs that didn't quite want to work right. He *really* needed to go.

The facility room was small with a tiny antigrav toilet and hand washer alongside the glass doors to a sonic shower that took up fully half of the space.

Aubrey relieved himself only to have his dick suddenly pulse to erection so fast his head went light, and his knees very nearly buckled. He grabbed onto the wall to keep from keeling over and stared down at himself. *What the . . .*

The swelling increased until even his balls ached, painfully.

Aubrey hissed and grabbed himself. The sensation from his own hand was so intense it practically burned. His head emptied of all thought but one, the need for relief. Hastily he spat on his hand and started stroking lightly, but quickly. Tension built ferociously fast—and held, and held, and held . . . He was right on the edge of explosion, but couldn't go over the edge.

Practically whimpering in frustration, he spat on both hands and tried again.

Nothing.

He tried stimulating his cock in every way his hands and fingers were capable of.

He couldn't cum.

Trembling, and very close to tears from the raw agony of frustration, he slid to his knees and set his head against the wall. "Fuck, fuck, fuck!"

The door opened and Seht stepped in. "Aubrey."

Aubrey looked up at him from the floor with his pants down around his knees and his swollen cock fully exposed and dripping.

Seht opened his pants, releasing his fully erect pair.

Aubrey's gaze focused on Seht's twin cocks and his mouth actually watered. Under his balls, something pulsed, hard. A fresh dribble of precum slid from the head of his cock.

Seht lifted one brow, but the feelings shimmering along their link was that of expectation.

Aubrey swallowed hard, then leaned forward onto his hands and turned around to face the wall on his hands and knees. He didn't give a shit about how humiliating it was. He knew to his bones that Seht would give him the relief he needed.

Soft steps sounded behind him. Fabric rustled. Cool fingers brushed along Aubrey's ass, then dug in, the nails scoring welts on his flesh that added to his urgency. A hot thick brand slid down the part between his cheeks and stopped, positioned against at the tight ring of his anus.

Yes, yes . . . Aubrey ducked his head and pressed back onto Seht's cock while straining to push outward and open himself. The ache of stretching to encompass the broad head felt damned good. *Gods, yes . . .*

Seht reached out to fist Aubrey's overlong hair and jerked his head back. He growled from his chest. "My pace, not yours, pet."

Trembling with desperation, the smallest of whimpers escaped Aubrey's throat. "Please?" His throat burned. He winced. Talking *hurt*.

Seht slammed in hard, fast, and perfectly on target.

The impact forced the air from Aubrey's lungs, but the stretch of fullness and the feeling of delicious pressure against that screamingly exciting spot deep within had him gasping for air just so he could moan it right back out in voluptuous carnal pleasure.

Seht groaned. The echo of pleasure burned across their link and rolled back and forth between them.

Aubrey shuddered, unbearably excited by the shared sensations. His interior muscles clenched greedily, and he writhed. *More . . . Please, more!*

Seht hissed in a breath, pulled back and thrust in, just as hard, just as fast, and just as on target. Barely a heartbeat passed, and he pulled back and thrust again, then again, and again, his hips slapping against Aubrey's ass in a fast staccato.

Aubrey panted while shoving back to meet him, but he wasn't quite able to keep up. Desperate hunger kept knocking him off rhythm.

Seht fell over his back and shoved Aubrey's head down onto the floor, forcing his body to hold still and merely receive.

Within Aubrey's belly, excruciating tension rose to a fever pitch, tightening his balls, and swelling his cock to painful urgency, forcing harsh gasps and moans from his throat. On the verge of screaming, his entire body tensed and released in a cascade of violent shudders. A scream spilled from his throat even as his body pumped itself out on the floor. His knees gave out under him and his body collapsed into his own spending.

Seht slid free of his body with a pained groan.

Panting, Aubrey turned to look up at him.

Seht stood to fasten his pants over his still erect cocks. "That should hold you until I get you back to bed."

Aubrey tried to rise from the floor, but his trembling arms wouldn't lift him from the floor. "You didn't . . . cum?"

"Relax, pet." Seht turned away to grab a disposable towel from the dispenser. He wet it carefully and turned back to Aubrey. "You've done enough for one day." Smiling, he knelt to clean up Aubrey's mess.

Seht wrestled Aubrey up from the floor and half carried, half dragged him back to the tiny round room. In what seemed to be the blink of an eye, Seht had them both undressed and under the covers. He fastened the cuff back around Aubrey's arm then pushing him over onto his side so he could spoon against Aubrey's back.

Aubrey sighed, more than ready to pass out.

Seht's hand closed on his upper thigh, pulled to lift it, and slid his legs between Aubrey's. The hot brand of Seht's cock pressed against Aubrey's anus. "Relax, pet."

He turned his head to get a glimpse of the pale boy behind him. "What . . ."

Seht thrust. His primary cock slid into Aubrey's body without a trace of resistance, even as his secondary cock slid under Aubrey's balls. He wrapped his arms around Aubrey, snuggling tight against his back. "Go to sleep, pet."

Aubrey frowned, shifting slightly against the fullness in his ass. "Sleep? But you . . ."

"Do not worry." Seht pressed a kiss to the base of Aubrey's neck, then slowly pressed deeper into him until something hard and round passed the loosened ring of Aubrey's anus. "I will find fulfillment. As we rest, your body will comfort mine, draining me slowly and extremely pleasurably."

Aubrey found it very difficult to keep his eyes open. "Okay."

The sound of a loud klaxon jerked Aubrey from a deep sleep. The bed shuddered under him.

Seht scrambled upright, his cock sliding wetly from Aubrey's body. "Stay here." He dragged on a pair of pants. "I will go see what is happening." Barefoot and shirtless, he slapped the wall to open it and lunged out from their room.

Alone in the small bed, Aubrey gripped the sheets under him trying to keep his heartbeat under control. He knew exactly what was happening. The ship was under attack. *Moribund . . .*

At the other end of the link, Seht's thoughts blazed with confidence. *Trust me, pet. Trust me to protect you.*

Trust wasn't something that came easily to Aubrey, but he wanted to believe in Seht. He *wanted* to . . ."Okay."

Twenty agonizing minutes later, the shuddering stopped.

Seht returned radiating with triumph and smiling with his fangs bared. "The pest that stupidly followed us is no more." He climbed into the bed, looked up, and tapped the ceiling right by the tube. Buttons appeared under his fingers. "No need for you to worry."

Aubrey felt something tingle in his wrist under the intravenous cuff he still wore.

Syrhus appeared in the room's small doorway. "Did you give him the sedative?"

Aubrey frowned. *Sedative?*

Seht turned to frown at his uncle. "Are you sure he needs one that strong?"

Aubrey felt lethargy begin to steal into his limbs.

Behind Seht's back, Syrhus lifted what appeared to be an extremely modern vapor syringe gun. "Yes." Viper fast, he reached in and grabbed Seht under the chin, tilting his head back.

Seht gasped and grabbed for Syrhus's wrist.

Syrhus applied the vapor syringe to the side of Seht's neck. There was a hiss marking its release. "I'm giving you the same dose." He pulled back, releasing the young prince.

Seht whirled around, but it was very plain to see that Seht's reflexes were already dragging. "Uncle?" He blinked and his knees trembled. He slid down the wall. "What . . ."

Syrhus took a deep breath and looked over at Aubrey. "I'm sorry, Seht, but you can't have him. He must be returned to his rightful owners."

Seht's eyes widened and his hands gripped the mattress under him. "Not to Moribund . . ."

Aubrey felt his heart trying to beat its way out of his chest. "No . . ." He would *not* go back to killing ships. He would *not* . . .

Syrhus shook his head. "No, not Moribund."

Aubrey felt the oddest wave of chill slide down his spine. If not Moribund, then who . . .

Seht growled low and vicious. "I'm his rightful owner! I caught him! I saved him! His life is mine!"

Syrhus shook his head. "He has a transmitter implanted in the back of his neck. Imperial Intelligence is already on their way to collect him."

A transmitter . . . Aubrey stared wide-eyed at Syrhus. Did he mean his penal chip?

Seht glared at Aubrey. *You knew you were wearing a transmitter?*

Aubrey frowned at Seht. *Moribund told me that he'd removed it* . . .

Seht shot a scowl at Aubrey. *Apparently, he lied.*

Aubrey frowned. *Then, how come the Agency didn't come after me before this?*

Seht rolled his eyes. *A ship can easily block or scramble an outgoing signal.* He turned his scowl back on his uncle. "When did you find out about this?"

"Just before the attack."

Seht shook his head. "A transmitter isn't that difficult to remove."

Syrhus shook his head. "It's explosive."

Seht stilled utterly, his eyes wide. "Explosive?"

Syrhus nodded. "I've also been informed that he possesses

a semi-active sleeper program in his interneural computational."

Aubrey frowned. "But I don't feel anything unusual."

Syrhus snorted. "Of course not. It is a sleeper program." He crossed his arms and casually leaned against the side of the oval doorway. "Diagnostics says that it is several years old and very deeply embedded."

What the hell could the Agency possibly have running in his head? He tried to think, but it was getting increasingly hard to hold his thoughts together. He was just too damned tired. His eyes drifted closed. He jerked them back open. This was no time to fall asleep! But he really, really wanted to.

Seht scowled at his uncle. "There has to be something we can do?"

Syrhus shook his head. "He must be returned."

Seht's eyes widened and panic began to shimmer under his thoughts. "No . . ."

"Yes." Syrhus's brows lowered and his gaze narrowed on Seht. "Until the Imperial Intelligence removes the transmitter and the program, your stray is too much of a danger to keep."

"He's mine." Seht's eyes drifted closed, then opened. He took a deep breath and spoke as firmly, but his body was already relaxing into a sprawl. "Properly registered. My pet. My . . . Aubrey."

Syrhus nodded. "Don't worry, in thirty days your stray will be safe enough to collect." He leaned in and reached past Seht to lift Aubrey's head.

Aubrey took a slow breath and spoke carefully. "Collect?"

Syrhus's brows rose. "You're still awake?" He smiled, showing his long teeth. "We have an entire division, one might say, devoted to the recovery of lost . . . pets."

Aubrey felt a strange buzz at the back of his neck, and a slight tug around his throat. Suddenly there was an . . . absence in his mind. Seht was gone. He couldn't feel him among his thoughts. A cold wash of panic washed through him. "Seht?"

Seht stared back at him with wide unfocused eyes. "Aubrey?"

Syrhus leaned back holding the silver collar. He shoved it into his belt, then caught Seht under his arms and lifted him from the small alcove.

His blue eyes wide and moist, Seht moaned struggled weakly, reaching back into the alcove. "Aubrey . . ."

Aubrey fought to raise his arm and reach for Seht, but it was just too damned hard. A whimper escaped his throat.

Syrhus smiled. "Don't worry. The two of you won't be separated for long." With the moaning Seht cradled against his chest, the long white mane falling over his arm, Syrhus turned to stare directly into Aubrey's eyes. "A *rehkyt* cannot hide among humans for very long. Not even one that is only half-turned. His, eyes, his teeth, his very blood will give him away." He strode away, taking Seht with him.

Pain swelled in Aubrey's heart and his eyes burned. He was being turned over to the Agency. His indenture was complete, so he'd be sent home. He'd be able to see Dad again. He should be thrilled, but all he could feel was the absence in his mind and his heart where Seht had been. He stared down the empty hallway until his eyes became impossibly hard to keep open.

Aubrey awoke to bright lights, loud voices and a strange burning hunger in his belly. "Seht?" His throat no longer hurt, but exhaustion dragged at him, rendering his voice to barely a whisper.

Someone patted his shoulder and spoke in a soft, deep voice. "Relax, you're going to be all right, son. You're on the Agency sweeper, *Machiavellian*. You're safe now."

Aubrey looked up and saw beeping and flashing

equipment everywhere. He was in some kind of hospital bay.

A man with a chiseled face smiled down at him. He wore a plain black uniform and his pitch-black hair was pulled back into a severe braid. He was quite obviously an Imperial intelligence agent. "You're healing very quickly. We've already downloaded the information and lifted the block on your memories. A few good meals and some thorough rest will have you back to . . . eh . . ." His smile faded, then reappeared. "You'll be up and around very soon."

Aubrey tried to concentrate on what he'd been told, but he was so tired.

Chapter Fifteen

Aubrey snapped awake in a very small room on a very small bunk. He sat up slowly, the blankets rolling down his chest. On the fold-down bunk across from him was a battered black duffel bag that he recognized. It was his dad's.

Memory crashed down on him. Suddenly his head was crammed full of things he hadn't recalled in several years.

The hijacking programs in his head were his own design, but he hadn't used them to steal ships to joyride, he'd made them to help his retired marine father in his salvage operation.

His father was dead, killed by the Moribund Company when they'd hijacked his freighter.

He hadn't been arrested by the Agency. Fueled by burning anger over his father's death, he'd volunteered to go deep undercover specifically to find the Moribund Company. The sleeper program was a lucid memory program that recorded everything that had happened to him. He had become a living, breathing recording device that utilized his ability to crack codes to tap into ships and record every operation, program, and code used in, on, or around him.

His father was dead.

He rose from the bunk and walked over to the duffel bag. Atop it lay a neatly folded pair of pants, a black t-shirt, and undergarments. Standard issue boots were tucked neatly under the cot. He carried the clothes into the small bathing room attached to his tiny cabin to take a shower.

His father was dead.

His heart ached with the knowledge, but the tears rolling

down his cheeks were for another absence entirely.

At the very end of the narrow steel-walled hallway, the black-uniformed yeoman knocked on the plain unmarked steel.

"Enter."

The yeoman opened the door and bowed, ushering Aubrey into a darkly appointed and heavily shadowed ready room. The carpets were black, as were the chairs and the broad desk that commanded the center of the room.

The man behind the desk stood. He was painfully slender with sleek black hair pulled tightly back into a long, slender braid. His rich amber brown eyes burned with intelligence in a face that looked hewn from stone. "Aubrey, welcome back."

Aubrey stepped into the center of the room and saluted. This time he recognized the tall, severe man. "Captain Sear."

Sear arched a fine black brow. "Civilians don't need to salute, Aubrey."

Aubrey froze. "Civilian . . ."

Sear sighed. "I'm afraid that I must release you from the Agency, with full honors of course." He rolled his eyes. "Not to mention a whole shitload of backpay."

Aubrey's mouth fell open. *Release me?* "But . . . why?"

Sear dropped back into his chair. "Simply put, you're no longer a citizen of the Empire."

Aubrey scowled, unconsciously bearing his long teeth. "What kind of crap is that?"

Sear's golden eyes narrowed. "According to medical, you've been genetically altered into a Skeldhi *rehkyt.*"

Aubrey frowned. "Yeah, so . . ."

"So . . ." Sear folded his arms across his chest. "According to our treaty with the Skeldhi, that makes you their legal possession and legally dead to the Empire."

Aubrey felt a cold wind blow around his heart even as a

growl welled up. "Are you going to send me back?"

Sear tilted his head to the side. "Do you want to go back?"

Aubrey shook his head. He had joined the Agency specifically to destroy the Moribund Company, and that was exactly what he planned to do, with or without the Agency's blessing. "I don't deal well with collars."

Sear nodded. "In that case, I seem to recall a mercenary craft that could use a first officer that knows how to talk to ships."

Aubrey stiffened in shock. "Mercenary . . ."

Sear leaned forward and folded his hand together on his desk. "Through your fine efforts, we have uncovered that the Moribund Company has an extremely highly placed . . . patron. This means that they cannot be dealt with directly through official channels, not even by the Agency. However, a mercenary destroyer is another story entirely." He smiled. "Sound interesting?"

Aubrey smiled right back. "It does."

Sear nodded. "In that case, you might want to consider using some of that back pay to make a few . . . cosmetic adjustments to conceal some of your less than human characteristics."

Aubre's jaw tightened, though his smile remained. "I plan to, among other things." *Lots of other things.*

Only days later, Aubrey left the *Machiavellian* on a tiny courier craft that flew on broad solar sails heading for a covert Agency clinic located deep in the heart of an asteroid.

A few days after that, he left the clinic on yet another courier ship with his fangs filed down to human flatness. He could finally chew his food again, instead of being forced to swallow it whole.

A week later, he arrived at a tiny outpost with another covert clinic. Two days later, he left with the points of his ears clipped down to human roundness. At the next clinic, his golden eyes were exchanged for those of silvery electrum with deep-space piloting augmentation. In still another clinic located in an isolated space station, he received biomechanical arm enhancements. After a particularly long shuttle jaunt, he arrived on a backwater planet and received augmentations to his legs.

Aubrey stared at his reflection in the small sanitary cubical attached to his cabin. Somewhere between hospital jaunts, his body gained in height and increased in muscle mass until he actually looked the age he was. At the same time, the golden sheen of his skin faded until he merely looked tanned. However, the dark waves of his hair remained tinted with deep red. He was not human, but the tall, broad-shouldered man that he saw in his mirror with gleaming silver eyes certainly looked human.

Another saying from his father came to mind. *Adapt, overcome.*

He nodded at his reflection. He was adapting. He *would* overcome. Moribund would pay for what he did.

After a very long jaunt in another solar sail courier vessel, he arrived on a distant colony world that was very nearly solid forest.

At the bottom of the courier ship's steps, a lean, broad-shouldered man greeted him. He had long deep red hair, elegantly pointed ears, and gold-green eyes that were cat-slitted. He smiled with fangs. "So, you're going to try hiding in plain sight?"

Aubrey's brows rose. *He smells like . . .* He smelled like himself. The man was a *rehkyt* in hiding.

The man nodded. "Greetings, cousin." He waved his arm toward the forest. "Ready to learn how to actually use that body of yours?"

Aubrey nodded firmly and followed him into the trees.

For almost an entire year, he trained in a form of sword and dagger fighting, and hand to hand combat that involved spectacular leaps. While training in survival techniques, he learned that certain animals, normally poisonous to humans, were in fact quite edible to *rehkyt*, and how to identify them by scent. He also learned that his severe allergic reaction to plant-based foods was genetic. The Skeldhi were strictly meat eaters, and so were the *rehkyt* they made. If it was green, it was damned near poisonous to him.

He came back out of the forest alone and boarded a shuttle. On board, he exchanged his forest leathers for breeches, a silk shirt with matching cravat, and a silver trimmed blue waistcoat. His overgrown mane was neatly trimmed to just below his shoulders and tied back with a black ribbon. Spit-polished boots were set on his feet. He shrugged into the royal blue long coat and belted on the sword of a first officer. Less than an hour after lift-off, he stepped on board the demon-class dreadnaught, *Reaper,* to report for duty to Captain Maria Melchior.

Finally, his very personal mission to wipe the Moribund Company from existence had begun.

However, in one particular area did his true *rehkyt* nature prove very difficult to adapt to, or overcome . . .

The stunning woman sitting behind the desk perused the file on her holographic projection monitor and tugged on the lapel of her snug maroon jacket. "Well, Aubrey, this is quite a situation we have here."

He curled his lip, revealing neat white, flat teeth. "I would appreciate it if you did not use *that* name, doctor."

"Oh?" She lifted her dark chocolate eyes and pursed her full sensual lips. "What would you prefer to be called?"

He held her gaze. "Ravnos will do."

She blinked then with a tilt of her head, and a toss of her

mass of red-cold curls that sent them tumbling over one shoulder, she slid her gaze out from under his and smiled brightly. "Very well then . . ." She lifted her chin, took a deep breath, lifting the ruffles of her pale gold low-necked blouse that framed her full breasts to perfection. "The captain tells me, Ravnos . . ." Her sultry gaze met his for a brief instant. "That you seem to prefer your pleasure with a little pain added to the mix."

He smiled sourly, folded his arms, and leaned back in the plush chair. "You could say that." *Stupid sex-drive . . .* He had no problems attracting lovers. He just couldn't *keep* them. No one wanted a lover that simply couldn't be gentle.

No one wanted a lover incapable of ever loving them in return either.

She looked over at him and lifted a brow. "The captain also told me that if your needs are left too long unsatisfied, you become rather . . . destructive."

He winced and looked away. It seemed that someone had finally noticed his occasional bar brawls with off-duty marines. Probably because he kept winning them. *Stupid marines . . .* With all the heavy-duty arm and leg augmentations marines had implanted, one would *think* they knew how to fight.

She tapped a perfectly manicured nail on the desktop. "Lethally destructive."

He winced. Apparently, the sword-duels he'd been participating in, and sometimes instigating on random space stations hadn't gone unnoticed either.

A soft masculine voice whispered across his memory. *"Sex or blood . . ."*

She folded her hands together and smiled. "And so we come to why you are here."

He lifted one dark brow. "The captain thinks I need a shrink?"

She shook her head. "I'm not a psychiatrist. I am a

therapist, a sexual therapist."

He choked on a laugh that wanted to be a scream. "Therapy can't fix this." He swallowed. "My aggression is . . . genetic."

She rolled her eyes. "No one wants to fix you. You're not broken. Trust me, I've seen broken, and you're nothing like that." She smiled. "I'm here to show you how to direct all that wonderful sexual aggression into safer channels."

His brows lifted. *Huh?* He shook his head. "You don't understand, I hurt people when I fuck them. In fact, I can't seem to get off unless I cause them some kind of pain."

She rose from her chair, revealing an extremely short and very tight skirt. "And what you don't understand, my dear young man, is that some of us can't get off *without* pain."

He frowned. "Isn't that a little . . . abnormal?"

She shook her head. "Less so than you might think. You simply need to find a lover that will match your need to *give* pain, with their need to *receive* pain."

He clutched the arms of his chair. "But I don't want to hurt anybody!"

She tilted her head and winked. "If pain brings them joy, where's the hurt?"

He shook his head. "This isn't making sense."

She smiled broadly. "Which is precisely why I am here. Tell me, Ravnos, have you ever spanked someone?"

"Huh?" He frowned. "As in, slapped their ass with my hand? Like a child?"

She chuckled. "I'll take that as a no." She pulled off her jacket.

He shrank back into his chair. "What are you doing?"

"Administering therapy." She tugged up her skirt showing stockings that ended at the top of her thighs and silky white panties. "Would you be so kind as to turn your chair to the side?"

He turned his chair, interested and somewhat aroused, in spite of himself. His dick was already at half-mast. "What are you planning to do?"

"I am going to lie across your lap, and you are going to smack my ass. You are going to smack it hard enough to make it nice and red, and then we will go from there."

He blinked and felt the blood rush downward to swell his cock. He *wanted* to smack her ass. "How hard?"

"Hard enough to make a nice clean handprint." She tossed him a grin. Preferably several."

CHAPTER SIXTEEN

On his twenty-first birthday, in the austere stateroom of the Agency sweeper *Machiavellian*, Commander Aubrey Ravnos removed his royal blue first officer's coat. With quick efficient movements, he slipped his arms into a black and silver captain's greatcoat marked with the insignia of the demon-class dreadnaught, *Hellsbreath*.

Captain Maria Melchior of the demon-class dreadnaught, *Reaper*, lifted a sheathed silver chased, live-steel sword and held it up cross-wise, presenting it to Ravnos.

Ravnos accepted the sheathed blade marked with his new ship's insignia with a slight bow, then buckled the sword-belt over the floor-length black coat.

The coat and weapon were holdovers from a more romantic time when ships sailed the seas rather than the stars. However, instead of the archaic tempered steel of the original officer's saber, the live-steel of Ravnos's mimetic blade practically hummed with nanites. The sword would return to shape from a forty-five-degree bend, would never lose its edge, and could withstand extremes in temperature, such as the absolute cold of space, without shattering. It would hold the perfect shape of its making for as long as it existed. Live-steel was said to be born, not made.

Captain Sear of the *Machiavellian*, and Captain Melchior lifted their champagne glasses in quiet ceremony.

Ravnos lifted the delicate champagne glass in acknowledgement of their toast. Once upon a time, he'd been little more than a half-wild kid struggling with strange drives and stranger urges. It had been quite a struggle, but at last, his life was orderly, perfectly under his control, and filled with purpose.

Captain Sear flopped onto the plush black leather couch and set his booted feet on the smoked-glass table before him. Starlight from the broad window behind him, showing open space, sparkled on his mirror-shined boots. "So, now that you're a respectable captain . . ."

Ravnos snorted. "Since when is a pirate, *respectable*?"

Captain Sear waved his gloved hand. "You're a privateer, a mercenary for legitimate hire, not a pirate out for his own gain."

Captain Melchior lifted the long skirts of her royal blue captain's coat and dropped into the matching recliner by the couch. "I'd say that's debatable." She grinned, and the dim golden light burnished her dark skin with copper highlights. Her pitch-black lion's mane of hair gleamed blue with only the slightest touch of silver. One dark brow lifted. "I think Ravnos gains plenty, every time Moribund loses another base to our guns."

From his seat on the opposite recliner, Ravnos nodded solemnly. "I gain one more peaceful night of sleep."

Captain Sear rolled his eyes. "Don't we all?"

Their shared laughter was quiet and subdued.

"Anyway . . ." Captain Sear sat up and slapped his black clad knees. "So, Captain Ravnos, how do you feel about a diplomatic mission?"

Ravnos blinked. "Diplomatic?"

Captain Sear nodded. "I have a highly sensitive document that needs to be delivered to Barbados Prime, just past Imperial borders."

Ravnos's brows lifted. Barbados Prime was the capital of the Republic of the Caribbean Stars, one of the richest and best defended star-based nations in the known universe. They were infamous for being the original safe-haven for the first space-flight privateers and merchant marine corps and had named their worlds for their most lucrative profession: interstellar piracy.

Over a century ago, the Republic had chosen to join the Imperial League of Interstellar Nations as a legitimate government and had supposedly stopped their plundering. Officially, they maintained their current level of wealth by training and deploying private armies that flew to engagements in Demon-Class Mercenary Warships. The small Republic was treated with sincere respect in the Empire, as not one Imperial House wanted the Republic's warships aimed at them.

Ravnos shook his head. "Do I want to know what this . . . document entails?"

Captain Sear shrugged. "They are your ship's articles declaring your fealty to President William Ayden Cyrus Kidd, of the Republic of Caribbean Stars. As they are a free government, you and your ship will be outside of Imperial jurisdiction."

Ravnos's smile tightened. "And beyond the reach of Moribund's extremely high placed patron, I assume?"

Captain Sear's pale lips stretched into a broad smile, baring his teeth. It wasn't exactly a pretty sight. "President Kidd utterly loathes the Moribund Company."

Captain Melchior rolled her expressive black eyes. "Oh great, you're cutting him loose in the rum and gambling capital of the known universe?"

Ravnos grinned. "You know, I always wanted to have my home port in paradise."

Captain Melchior narrowed her gaze on Ravnos. "Don't go marrying any professional courtesans."

Ravnos blinked. "Are you saying I should marry an amateur?"

"Oh!" Sear lifted one black-gloved finger and grinned.

"That reminds me . . ." He leaned to one side to reach into his coat pocket. "I have a gift for you." He pulled out a flat white paper box the size of his hand. He flicked his wrist and sent the box spinning toward Ravnos.

Ravnos reached out and snagged the flying box. "A gift?"

Sear's smile widened to show his teeth. "Open it."

Ravnos opened the box and lifted out a gold bangle as thick as his pinky. "A bracelet?" His augmented vision focused on the shimmering iridescence moving along the metal. The band was covered . . . no, made of titanium nanites. "This is . . . mimetic?"

Sear chuckled. "Keyword, anchor thirteen."

Ravnos frowned at the band in his palm. "Anchor thirteen." The band promptly shrunk down to a width of three fingers, the perfect size for a . . . Ravnos looked over at Sear. "A cock-ring?"

Sear shrugged. "Well, you *are* going to be stationed in the rum and gambling capital of the known universe." He lifted his glass of champagne. "Wouldn't want you to lose control right away."

Captain Melchior threw back her head and released a peal of laughter. "Perfect!"

*

From his window seat in the *Hellsbreath's* extremely posh captains' gig, Ravnos looked down on the sprawling capital city of the Republic of the Caribbean Stars. The vast collection of pillared, whitewashed, palazzos were perched on the very edge of the rugged cliffs overlooking the seacoast. The gold, silver, and copper plated domes sparkled under iridescent energy deflection domes. The surrounding ocean was a perfect turquoise blue, and the sandy coast a snowy white under the planet's double sun. Imported Terran palm trees waved their broad fronds in the near constant sea breeze.

It was the very picture of paradise.

The barque veered toward the broad cone of the space dock.

Ravnos settled back into his seat. He had wanted to spend his entire two weeks of shore leave in the city, but that simply wasn't possible. It seemed that he wasn't the only one with an appointment with President Kidd. According to his intelligence, there were several visiting dignitaries, including an Imperial admiral and a royal delegation from Skeldhor.

Seht . . . Ravnos pressed a hand over his pounding heart. He took a deep, slow breath and reached for calm. There was no way in hell that Seht would be there.

But if he was . . .

He shook his head firmly. He had no intention of being anywhere close enough to them to find out. He would not endanger his dream of annihilating the Moribund Company with even the remote possibility that he might be recognized for what he was. Not even for the chance to catch a glimpse of the one person that still haunted his dreams.

The *Hellsbreath's* gig eased over the mile-wide mouth of the cone-shaped spaceport sliding into the Meissner antigrav inertial-dampening field. Bells sounded, warning all other ships that the gigantic superconductors miles below under the floor of the pit were in use. The ship drifted downward.

Eyes closed, Ravnos monitored everything through his residual link to the gig's sentience. His nav-pilot and the small craft worked in perfect sync, the organic mind blending seamlessly with the machine's sentience. He nodded in approval.

Synchronization didn't always happen. More than a few pilots treated the ships they flew as dead unthinking objects. Not a good idea, when more often than not, the ship was far more intelligent and in the case of the larger, older ships, salient or self-aware. Salient ships were more than capable of point-blank refusing to fly for a pilot. God help the pilot that succeeded in pissing their ship off. Snowfall in their private quarters was the least an annoyed ship was capable of.

At the appropriate level, the gig's descent stopped and the small craft's electro-turbines kicked in to nudge the gig to the side and into their assigned dock. The gig settled gently into its birth. Behind them, the gigantic ramp that led into the pit lifted and closed, cutting off the influence of the gravity field. His men scrambled to prepare for debarking.

Ravnos rose from his seat, straightened his coat, and headed for the pressure door a yeoman held open.

His lieutenant and three of his six-man crew preceded him down the short flight of stairs and assembled at the foot.

He stepped down to the bottom of the staircase. The air was warm and fragrant with flowers, even as deep as they were in the space dock.

As one, his men's hands rose to the polished bills of their caps in salute. Their black and silver uniforms were pressed to crisp perfection, and their spit-shined knee boots gleamed under the dock lights. Each carried a live-steel saber at their side, but no side-arm. No soldier walked without a weapon at his side, but in the vacuum of space where a single pinhole through a ship's hull could be enough to kill everyone on board, projectile and energy weapons were too dangerous to allow on any ship.

An elegant and crushingly expensive silver antigrav limousine floated into the dock propelled by nearly silent electro-turbines. It settled only ten paces from the gig's staircase.

Ravnos contemplated the sleek vehicle with a frown. "Nav-pilot." The receiver sensor fastened to his collar vibrated a tiny amount.

The nav-pilot's voice crackled from his earcom. "Yes, Captain?"

Ravnos folded his hands behind him. "There's a . . . vehicle in our berth."

"Yes, Captain, transportation courtesy of the president."

Ravnos's brows lifted. *The president?* He was only a ship captain, not a royal dignitary. He shook his head. "Thank you, Nav-pilot."

"Aye, aye, Captain."

Crap . . . Ravnos signaled his men to begin loading his belongings and the crate of gifts intended for the president. He didn't want to chance that he might insult the president by refusing. However, he wasn't about to leave his escort behind either, not with both an Imperial admiral and a Skeldhi delegation in residence.

He turned to his lieutenant. "Follow me in the *Imp*. Once we disembark, keep it manned, and within one minute range of my signal at all times. Tell the men to stay on alert and in contact with each other through the secure frequency." He seriously considered telling them to strap on their body armor, but he didn't think that would make a good impression on his high-ranking host. This called for subtlety. Ravnos lifted his chin. "And, have the men wear a deflection scarab."

When activated, the small oval device projected a nearly invisible energy field around the wearer. It wouldn't stop a bolt at point-blank range, but it would deflect sword slashes, knife thrusts, and anything fired from beyond two body-lengths away. It was commonly worn by security personnel and street constables, so it shouldn't be too offensive.

The lieutenant's brows lifted. "Expecting trouble?"

Ravnos smiled grimly. "Merely a precaution."

The lieutenant tugged on the polished brim of his hat and bowed briefly. "Aye, aye, Captain." He turned and hurried back to the gig. The rest of the crew followed on his heels.

Only moments later, a flat black, deflection plate armored transporter with long, narrow, and heavily tinted windows along the sides, eased out from the rear dock of the gig.

Ravnos lowered himself into the plush back seat of the

limousine. The automatic door closed behind him.

The limousine's spinning turbines powered up, lifting the sleek expensive vehicle from the pavement. Emitting only a soft hum, it eased from the dock and turned onto the broad curving roadway that circled the inertial shield wall holding the powerful Meissner field within the central pit. Within minutes, the limousine followed by the black transport with his crew sped from the cone-shaped space dock and down the broad roadway that ran along the spectacular coastline.

Ravnos settled back into the seat and sighed. He'd assumed that his rank as a mere ship's captain meant he'd be granted a short office visit to deliver his papers and perhaps a private word or two. The limousine was an ominous sign. He rubbed his brow. *I hope this doesn't mean I'm going to have to attend some kind of state dinner or other silly formal function.* His table manners were okay, but chefs tended to get upset when they realized that he wouldn't touch any dish with even a hint of green vegetables.

The gleaming silver limousine rose from the coastline roadway, turned landward, and soared toward the gleaming domes at the heart of the capital city. The plain black transport followed close behind. With smooth precision, they eased into the stream of flight-traffic heading into the city, accompanied by a vast array of streamlined civilian vehicles and bulky utilitarian commercial transports.

Sunlight shimmered in rainbow hues on the plasti-steel windows and gleamed on the metallic domes and marbled pillars of the old-world classical-style buildings. The windows, balconies, walkways, and arches of every home and shop were overrun with climbing flowers in every conceivable color. The people that walked the winding streets were tanned a golden brown and wore layered robes in as many colors as the flowers that grew everywhere. It made an interesting contrast against ultra-modern chrome and smoked-glass corporate districts.

On the far edge of the island, they approached a sprawling palatial complex of domes overrun with trees and flowers. At the very center rose a sleek tower that appeared to be made of glass. Balconies overrun with flowers and plants dotted the entire structure. As they drew closer, he suddenly realized that what he had taken for balconies were, in fact, broad landing platforms nearly forested with huge flowering trees. The tower was monstrous at nearly two meters wide.

The limousine and the transporter passed through a shimmering energy field and drifted toward the mid to lower levels, then settled down onto one of the smaller landing platforms, the size of four city blocks. The limousine door opened.

Ravnos stepped out into bright sunshine and a warm sea breeze. The view was spectacular. From where he stood, he was able to see the coastline of almost the entire island.

A young gentleman in a bright blue frock coat and knee breeches approached from the glass double doors. His feathered tricorn hat sat atop curling black hair that was tied back at his nape with a broad blue bow. His entire ensemble was practically dripping with frothy white lacy. He bowed. "Welcome to Barbados Prime, Captain Ravnos. I am Toggs, chamberlain to the president." He turned to the side and waved a hand toward the open doors beyond. "The president is waiting for you."

Ravnos, his lieutenant, and four of his crew followed Toggs through the double doors and along curving carpeted hallways with floor to ceiling windows along one side. Ravnos couldn't help but stare at the panoramic view.

Toggs stopped at a pair of mirrored doors that parted to reveal a lift. Long minutes passed on the rising lift marked by Terran classical instrumental music. The lift finally stopped, and the mirrored doors parted.

Ravnos stepped out into a broad and expansive round room. The floor, the distant curving walls, and the pillars that marched all the way around the room were cream marble flecked with gold. His gaze was drawn from the extravagant and blatantly erotic statues stationed between the pillars, and then upward to the gigantic mural that spread across the domed ceiling overhead. It featured two ancient sailing ships engaged in a sea battle during a storm. Ravnos's brows lifted. Apparently, the president was quite fond of his ancient history.

Toggs stepped to the side. "Please go in, Captain Ravnos, however, I would ask that your men remain by the door."

Ravnos tilted his head at his lieutenant.

The lieutenant signaled to his men, and the four crewmen split into two pairs and took position on either side of the door.

The president's chamberlain nodded.

Ravnos turned and strode down the carpeted runner toward the far end of the room and the golden oak desk perched on an exotic Terra-Persian styled rug.

Behind the desk sat a man in a gold frock coat, his long blond hair tied back with an extravagant cream bow. Directly behind him, two guards stood at attention. Despite their seemingly frivolous dark blue frock coats trimmed in black lace, there was no mistaking that both guards were marine augmented. They held tall polearms tipped with blades that crackled faintly, revealing that they were, in fact, electromagnetic weapons designed specifically to fry an attacker's mechanical augmentations.

Standing before the desk stood a tall, slender figure entirely swathed in a frost-white hooded cloak.

The man behind the desk leaned back in his chair and smiled up at the figure before him. "I will allow you passage to search for your missing . . . person."

The cloaked figure sketched a small bow. "Thank you, President Kidd . . ."

"However . . ." The man behind the desk lifted a cautionary finger. Lace frothed from his wide gold coat cuffs. "You may not collect him without his verbal consent."

The figure in white stiffened. "What . . ."

The president smiled and folded his hands together. "You said yourself that he's not a criminal, but someone you care deeply for."

"Yes, but . . ."

The president tilted his head to the side. "Then why would he not consent to leaving with you?"

The figure in white took a step back, bowed stiffly, then straightened. "I accept your terms."

The president nodded and his smile broadened. "Good luck on your . . . hunt."

Ravnos slowed his steps. Something about the hooded figure in white was making his heart slam in his chest, but it didn't feel like fear. It felt more like . . . anticipation.

The figure whirled around in a swath of white silk, revealing a pale masculine face carved in exotic lines with high cheekbones and delicately pointed ears. His full lips were drawn into a tight line and his electric blue eyes burned with intensity. A long slender snow-white braid fell over the shoulder of his black iridescent, body-hugging ship-suit to tumble past his waist. A plain and very business-like sword was belted at his hip. Gleaming black boots rode all the way up to his thighs.

He was painfully beautiful, and definitely Skeldhi.

Ravnos stiffened. *Oh, crap . . .*

The Skeldhi's long strides carried him back down the carpeted walkway straight toward Ravnos.

Ravnos continued forward staring dead ahead, his gaze firmly on the distant wall and away from the other man's eyes.

The man marched past Ravnos, the white cloak brushing

against the hem of Ravnos's long black coat.

Ravnos took a completely unintentional breath. The rich scent of the man walking past him filled his nose and lifted every hair on his body. He knew that scent. He knew this man. Heat coursed all the way through him, and sheer shock spilled in cold waves that lifted the hair on his body. *Oh my God . . . Seht?* Somehow, he continued to walk forward without the slightest hint of the vertigo spilling through his limbs.

Behind him, the lift pinged, indicating that the doors had closed, carrying the Skeldhi prince elsewhere.

Ravnos very nearly walked into the desk before him. He stopped, startled at his sudden arrival.

The man seated behind the desk tilted his head, one golden brow lifted. "Captain Ravnos, I presume?"

CHAPTER SEVENTEEN

Standing before the gracefully carved golden oak desk, Ravnos bowed to the President of the Republic of the Caribbean Stars. "President Kidd." His expression was perfectly neutral despite the fact that it felt as though a fist had closed tight around his heart. He utterly refused to even consider that the painful ache attempting to choke off his breath had anything to do with the fact that Seht had brushed up against him and had not noticed him.

The man behind the broad desk rose to his feet, resplendent in an ornate cream and gold frock coat and waistcoat that was tied closed with a pale cream sash. The entire outfit was practically encrusted with gold embroidery and cream seed pearls. His spun-gold hair was drawn back from his pale brow and bound at the nape of his neck with a cream silk bow, the long wavy tail tumbling to his waist. A full head and a half shorter than Ravnos, the president was forced to lift his chin to meet Ravnos's gaze. Golden brows swept up over electric blue eyes. The smile on his lips was both welcoming and a touch sly. "Goodness, I sincerely hope that our clearly less than adequate doorways are not proving difficult for your . . . stature?"

Ravnos stared down at the far smaller and slighter man. He schooled his expression to perfect blandness. "I've managed not to dent too many of the lintels, sir."

The president chuckled and held out a white-gloved hand, a froth of cream lace tumbling from his broad coat cuff. "I've heard many fine things about you, Captain."

Ravnos's dark brows lifted. "Oh?" He lifted his black leather gloved hand and gripped the hand offered carefully. "You've heard that I'm a blood-thirsty battle-commander with an extremely nasty temper when crossed?"

The president's smile broadened. "As I said, many fine things." He released Ravnos's hand. "I'm more than pleased to offer you and your ship a safe harbor."

Ravnos nodded and relaxed enough to smile. "I couldn't have wished for a better place to call home, President Kidd." He reached into the breast pocket of his waistcoat and withdrew a tiny data crystal. He held it out to the president. "My charter, sir."

The youthful president took the tiny crystal and slipped it into his own inner breast pocket. He tilted his head and lifted a golden brow. "Would you object to the occasional private mission, between hunting forays?"

Ravnos didn't even blink. That the president might offer him a side job or two was expected. He would have been far more surprised if the president hadn't asked for such. "That would be perfectly acceptable, sir."

The president clasped his hands and nodded. "I'm very glad to have you with us." He tilted his head, and his blue eyes narrowed. "The enemy of my enemy is my friend, no?"

Ravnos stilled utterly. *Seht* . . . He shook it off with a slight smile. "My father said the very same thing."

The president nodded. "He sounds like an intelligent man."

"He was." Ravnos's mouth tightened.

The president's brows lifted, then fell. He nodded. "I see; my condolences."

Ravnos's smile gentled. "Appreciated."

The president inclined his head, then smiled. "Now then . . ." He tugged at the lace falling from his cuffs. "I will send my aide to you with the particulars of where you will be stationed. A small private estate has been prepared for you and your crew's convenience. I also have a list of companies willing to take commission for recovery and repair for your ship, should you need them . . ."

Ravnos had only half his attention on the conversation. Truthfully, he was merely nodding at the appropriate lulls while internally recording what was said for later perusal. He was far more interested in who Seht was looking for in the Republic of the Caribbean Stars. The fist around his heart and the cold sweat sliding down his spine told him that he knew exactly who the Skeldhi prince sought. But why was the prince still perusing him after so many years? Why hadn't he just given him up?

A ping sounded, signaling that the lift doors behind him had opened.

A voice called out in the echoing room. "Sir, you must wait . . ."

"I do not . . . wait." The voice was cultured, soft, slightly mechanized and . . . familiar. Heavy boots thumped on carpet.

Ravnos stilled. Where had he heard that voice before? His internal computational automatically sorted through his monstrous collection of voice files, choosing and discarding voice track after voice track at the speed of thought. The closest match was . . . Memories flitted through his mind, of darkness and a medical table, then a floor, punctuated by faded echoes of screaming pain from . . . ice in his lungs.

Ravnos's eyes widened and his breath stilled. *Moribund . . .* But it couldn't be him . . . He schooled his expression to neutrality, showing only mild boredom, and turned very slowly.

The man striding up the carpet was tall, broad-shouldered, and refined in appearance. Perfectly groomed golden hair fell in graceful waves across a high brow. Neatly trimmed golden brows arched over sapphire blue eyes. His carved porcelain face was very nearly feminine with high cheekbones. He was the very picture of a high-ranking noble of the Imperial court, but he moved with the smooth refinement of the extremely, and expensively, augmented. Clearly, his body was more machine than man.

However, what held Ravnos's attention was that he wore a blindingly white, painfully tailored uniform practically encrusted with gold braid with a floor-sweeping cape and the long coat of a high-ranking Imperial officer. He frowned slightly at the man's insignia. *An admiral? That can't be Moribund.* He searched through his data files trying to match the face with a name.

"President Kidd . . ." The noble admiral stopped before the desk on Ravnos's immediate left. "A moment of your time, if you please?"

Ravnos lifted his brow. By standing on his left, the noble was blocking Ravnos's sword arm. *Rude bastard.*

The noble's gaze traveled across Ravnos's clearly mercenary uniform. He focused on the ship insignia displayed in silver and jet on the left breast of Ravnos's long coat. More than one iris shifted in the depths of his eyes, revealing that they were entirely artificial and designed for deep space. His gaze chilled, but his full mouth smiled almost sweetly. "You won't mind, will you?"

Ravnos's brows lifted. That was an interesting expression. He couldn't have reproduced it if he tried. "How does he do that?"

The president smiled. "You mean that disdainfully cheerful 'I hate your guts and plan to kill you, but don't trouble yourself over it' look?"

Ravnos blinked. He hadn't actually intended to say that out loud. On the other hand, he didn't mind joining the president in a small game of *'let's annoy the rude admiral by talking about him as if he's not there.'* Ravnos nodded. "Yeah, that." He tilted his head to glance at the agreeably sneering admiral, then turned to purse his lips thoughtfully at the president. "That must have taken quite some time to perfect."

Kidd rolled his eyes and shook his head. "I've been trying for ages, but I still can't quite get it." He winked at Ravnos. "I have a few council members I would dearly love to use it on."

Ravnos tucked his thumbs into his belt and smiled. "I could see how that might come in handy." His mental files suddenly coughed up an image of the man beside him.

Admiral Roth "Satan's Wrath" Moraine of the Angel class dreadnought *Righteous,* also known as the Emperor's Sword, in charge of the Imperium's largest fleet, fourth in rank from the throne, a prince of the third quadrant and twice decorated with the Imperial Star for heroism in battle.

"I am so pleased that my presence brings you such amusement." Admiral Moraine's voice was calm, cultured, and clicked into a perfect match with what Ravnos had recorded as Moribund.

Ravnos turned to stare at him. "I'll be damned . . ." *He is Moribund.* But how could he be the most wanted man in known space and also be . . .the hero of the Empire? *Something to think about later.* He tuned his entire mental array to memorizing everything he could about the man beside him, up to and including the exotic cologne that didn't quite disguise the scent of extremely expensive designer hydraulic fluid.

Admiral Moraine inclined his head slightly, his eyes crinkling at the corners with humor, but his lips curled back to show perfectly even teeth in what might assume was a smile, but according to the fine hairs on the back of Ravnos's neck, was, in fact, a snarl. "Ah, so you recognized me?"

Ravnos blinked. *That was the understatement of the century.* Was he telepathic? Only one way to find out. He curled back his lips in an exact replica of Moraine's snarling smile. "You're a celebrity. Kind of hard to miss . . ." *You murdering sack of shit.*

Admiral Moraine nodded absently. "Yes, thank you, now if you don't mind, Captain, I truly wish to have a private word with President Kidd?"

Ravnos released a soft breath. Nope, not telepathic, just a damned good guesser.

President Kidd waved his hand. "Of course you may have a private word!" He tapped the top of his desk. A holographic display bloomed into life a few inches above the surface of his desk. He frowned at the data flowing upward before him. "How does the twenty-third, at half past nine in the morning, sound to you?" He turned and smiled at the admiral.

The admiral's eyes widened. "Three days from today . . ."

President Kidd plastered on the sincerest look of regret that Ravnos had ever seen. "I'm sorry, but that's soonest I have available at the moment?" He shook his head sadly. "I'm booked solid until then."

Moraine shook his head. "I'm sure the Captain wouldn't mind . . ."

The president abruptly threw up his hands. "Oh yes, how thoughtless of me!" He set one hand behind his back and waved the other in Ravnos's direction. "Admiral Moraine, may I introduce Captain Ravnos, who was kind enough to agree to join my dreadnaught fleet."

Moraine blinked, his expression going completely blank for a millisecond, only to be replaced by a very charming smile of utter disdain. "Ah. Ravnos, originally of the dreadnaught, *Reaper,* under Captain Maria Melchior?"

Ravnos gave a short, curt bow. "I have that distinction."

Kidd nodded and smiled broadly. "He's an excellent battle-commander, particularly against Moribund Company ships."

Ravnos didn't quite flinch.

"So I'd heard." Moraine turned to regard Ravnos with wide eyes, yet a tight mouth. "Your pursuit of the Moribund

Company leads one to think there might be a personal vendetta involved." His brow lifted.

Ravnos smiled mildly. "Yes, one just might think that."

President Kidd clasped his hands before him. "My most abject apologies, but I really do need to complete this meeting with Captain Ravnos. I have yet another meeting directly after with one my senators."

The admiral eyed Ravnos, then lifted his chin to focus on the far smaller man behind the desk. "With all due respect, President, I really must insist."

"With all due respect, Admiral . . ." President Kidd set one gloved hand down on his desk. "*I* really must insist."

The president's guards took a simultaneous step forward, their bladed pole arms crackling with electricity.

Admiral Moraine inclined his head toward the president, turned on his heel in a perfectly executed 'about-face', then strode back down the carpet toward the lift.

Kidd's gaze narrowed, watching the admiral's progress.

Behind him, Ravnos heard the soft ping of the lift closing. He leaned over the desk and dropped his voice to a sub-tonal wavelength that normal sound detection equipment wouldn't detect. "President, this may sound crazy, but that man was Moribund."

The president nodded and leaned down to reply on the same sub-tonal wavelength. "I know."

Ravnos stilled. "What?" He stared at the President of the Republic of the Caribbean Stars. "How . . ."

Kidd smirked. "Let's just say that Agent Sear has a weakness for dark and bittersweet chocolate."

Sear knew . . . Ravnos's narrowed his eyes. "If the Agency knows, then why . . ."

Kidd waved his gloved hand and snorted. "Why doesn't someone just go to his house and arrest him?" He shook his head. "Unfortunately, Moribund is not merely the mastermind behind a highly organized crime syndicate, he's also fourth in line to the Imperial throne. There's not a damned thing anyone in your Imperium can do about him . . . *officially.*" He leaned close and his smirk returned. "Which is where you and I come in." He lifted a finger. "Which reminds me." He reached into his pocket and withdrew a neatly folded sheet of paper bearing a wax seal and ribbons.

Ravnos eyed the folded paper with deep suspicion.

President Kidd pressed it into Ravnos's hand and smiled. "You will attend tonight's dinner and musical, won't you?"

Crap . . . Ravnos hid his wince with a tight smile and a nod. "Of course, Mr. President."

CHAPTER EIGHTEEN

After a rather long ascending lift ride and a march through curving windowed hallways, Ravnos and his men arrived in the spacious four-bedroom suite that was their temporary quarters. Less than half an hour later, his four crewmen, led by his lieutenant, had his formal captain's attire unpacked, pressed, starched, and ready for donning the moment he stepped from the shower. One of his men had even taken the time to polish the two dozen silver buttons on his black velvet armored long coat while yet another had polished his boots to a mirror gloss.

Ravnos counted himself lucky that he was allowed to put on his own undergarments, stockings, and trousers.

His senior yeoman tucked his shirtsleeves into the armholes of his black brocade waistcoat, and then into the sleeves of his captain's coat, so as not to crush the starched perfection of his lace cuffs and collar. Ravnos was then allowed to don the shirt, waistcoat, and coat simultaneously, but forced to stand perfectly still while a yeoman buttoned his shirt and attended to his cufflinks. A lace cravat that was starched within an inch of its life was set around his collar and tied in a florid bow.

While this was happening, yet another yeoman combed his damp beyond-shoulder-length hair and rather firmly tamed it into a tightly braided queue tied with a black silk ribbon in an over-large bow. A broad silver sash was tied around him, and brushes were brought out to stroke the black velvet of his coat into sleek perfection. Finally, his ornate, black and silver

155

etched captain's sword-bearing *Hellsbreath's* crest was belted around him.

The four men stood back to intently peruse their handiwork.

Feeling rather put upon, Ravnos glared at them. "Am I presentable enough for you?"

The four crewmen looked over at the lieutenant.

The lieutenant tilted his head to either side and rubbed his jaw, his brows lifting in clear uncertainty. "Eh . . ." He grinned. "You'll do."

Ravnos rolled his eyes while positioning his arm-length parrying dagger at the small of his back. "Remind me again, why I let you bully me this way?"

His lieutenant stepped forward and pressed the handwritten invitation into Ravnos's hand. "Because you have yet to select a first officer to protect you from us."

Ravnos snorted and tucked the invitation into the wide cuff of his sleeve. "I'll make that my first priority."

His lieutenant nodded firmly. "See that you do." He then practically shoved his captain out of the suite and into the lift. "Have fun and play nice, Captain!" He waved while the lift doors eased closed.

In the solitude of the descending lift, Ravnos stared at the handwritten, wax-sealed, and beribboned command cleverly disguised as a formal invitation to dinner and allowed himself the luxury of a deep rumbling growl. "Play nice, my ass!" This was a disaster in the making; he could feel it. Not only would he have to 'play nice' with the Imperial Colonel that would undoubtedly be there, but he'd have to hide his intolerance to certain very common human foods; namely vegetables. An intolerance that would be very recognizable to the entire Skeldhi delegation who would most certainly be present.

He activated his communicator. "*Imp one*, are you in position?"

The ear com crackled. "Aye, aye, Captain, one minute from your signal."

Ravnos nodded. "Good. Out." Thank the fates he'd thought to prepare an escape plan, just in case. He fisted his hands to flex the muscles in his forearms, feeling for the throwing blades sheathed inside both of the sleeves of his captain's coat. All things considered, it was looking less like 'just in case,' and more like 'any second now.'

The elevator stilled. Several small and metallic things smacked against the door's exterior with ringing pops followed by the distinct and familiar scream of metal scoring metal.

Ravnos stiffened. That sounded like . . . bolt pistols? He whirled to the left and tucked himself against the side. The lift was too small to unsheathe his sword. *Piss!* His thumb pressed against the scarab on his belt. A slight hum and a barely visible wavering in the air around him marked the activation of the deflection field.

The doors parted. Smoke whirled into the lift reeking of scorched metal, melting stone, and copper sweet tang of blood. A cacophony of hoarse shouts, the ring of live-steel against live-steel, and the loud retort of hand-held bolt pistols hammered against his ears.

Ravnos freed his parrying dagger from its sheath at his back and peeked past the edge of the open lift doors. The hallway beyond was a merry hell of smoke, fire, and broken bodies wearing blood-spattered Imperial white and shattered exotic black armor. *What the hell . . .*

At the center of the maelstrom whirled the hulking and distorted shape of a blood-drenched, Marauder cyborg. Tusks curled from its screaming mouth. Its hands were fingered with knives as long as his forearm. Irregularly shaped scales coating the beast in bullet-repelling armor, and a long prehensile bladed tail swung in a deadly arc. It mowed through both the Imperial delegation and the sword-wielding Skeldhi with complete abandon.

Ravnos noted the tattered remains of the bright blue frockcoat of the president's chamberlain hanging from the creature's distorted shoulders and winced. *A sleeper assassin, fuck* . . . The fates only knew when the Marauder nano-virus was implanted in its unwitting and doomed host. The nano-virus was capable of remaining dormant for years, appearing as merely a bit of half-erased data. However, once the second half of the code was delivered, the host's own nanites transformed them physically, mechanically, and mentally, into a monstrous and deadly cyborg that would not cease tearing apart everything and everyone in its path until its target had been found and destroyed. Once its mission had been accomplished, the last string of code activated, reversing the transformation and killing its host in the process, leaving the victim to take the blame for the killing spree.

Ravnos narrowed his gaze and adjusted his eyesight to see through the smoky haze. Someone in that hallway had provided the activation code, and he had a damned good idea who.

A Skeldhi man in decorative armor, a sword in one hand and a long dagger in the other, hurtled backwards past the doors of the lift, his white hair flying like a flag. The man slammed into the wall and collapsed on the carpeted floor. He gasped for breath and shoved his long hair from his blood-spattered face with a gloved hand, leaving scarlet smears in his wake. Snarling something unintelligible, he rose to stand on unsteady feet, then marched back toward the fight, passing close by the open doors of the lift.

The barest trace of the scent of the man's anger-sweat brushed past Ravnos's sensitive nose. He stiffened. He knew that scent. *Seht!* Fire sparked at the base of Ravnos's skull. The world slowed down around him. His gaze narrowed on the man passing less than an arm-length away, the edges of his vision fading to a blur. With careless ease, he sheathed his weapons and reached out with his right hand to grab a handful of white hair, pulling Seht's head back. His left arm looped around the man's throat, tipping him backwards to tumble into the lift, and into his arms.

The man in his arms snarled and swung one hand down, jabbing his long dagger backwards. A nasty screech announced the blade's contact with Ravnos's deflection field cast by the scarab Ravnos wore on his belt.

The world slammed back into normal speed and Ravnos gasped in shock. What the hell had he just done? Of all the stupid, moronic, lame-brained, idiotic, and suicidal things to do . . .

Seht screamed and fought, kicking out with both feet.

Shit . . . Ravnos struggled to keep his balance while holding the struggling Skeldhi. He was forced to release the man's hair so he could clamp that arm around Seht's body, trapping his arms and the sword and dagger he held.

Seht's foot slammed into the lift's control panel, swinging them both into an inadvertent twist.

Ravnos's back slammed into the lift wall with a metallic crunch. His breath woofed from his lungs, but he held tight to the kicking and bucking Skeldhi prince. However, now that he had him, what in bleeding Fate was he supposed to *do* with him? He eyed the open lift doors. *I suppose I could just throw him back out . . .*

The doors closed and the lift shuddered into movement.

Ravnos winced. *Or not.*

"Human, you will die for this!" Seht threw his head back, clearly attempting a head-butt.

Ravnos dodged the head-butt and bared his teeth. Seht still didn't know him. He should have felt relieved, but for some monumentally stupid reason that he just couldn't fathom, it seriously pissed him off. He snarled right against Seht's ear.

"Pity I'm not human, eh?"

Seht froze.

Ravnos used that tiny pause to twist hard, turning them both completely around to smash Seht into the wall.

Seht turned his head to the right, barely in time to save his face and choked. He sucked in a ragged breath. "What . . ."

Ravnos growled in frustration. He was pressed right up against the man, but he couldn't feel a damned thing. The scarab's deflection field wouldn't let him actually make contact with Seht's body. He released Seht's throat to reach down to his belt and thumb the device off. Abruptly, his chest pressed into the man's solidly armored back, but his pelvis and his cock made full and glorious contact with Seht's firm backside.

Erotic fire seared him all the way up the back of his skull. A soft gasp escaped him. Heat flooded him and raced downward, filling his cock at breathtaking speed. He groaned in sheer lust. Seht's sleek muscular ass felt so damned good. He nosed under Seht's hair to breathe in the scent of his skin. *Bloody Fate, he smells fantastic.*

Seht twisted hard and snapped at him, venomous saliva dripping from his bared fangs. "What the hell do you think you're doing?"

Ravnos's gaze locked on the exposed right side of Seht's throat and the gentle pulse under the pale skin. "Here's a clue." He opened his mouth and clamped down hard on the side of Seht's neck. His fangs had been filed down, but the force of his bite was more than strong enough to break the tender skin. Sweet copper slid across his tongue. He released his bite to lap at the tears his front teeth had left behind.

Seht shuddered in Ravnos's arms and his eyes widened. "Venom . . ." His dark pupils dilated wide, the blue pushed back to become little more than slender rings around pits of darkness. "Your scent . . . *rehkyt?*"

Aubrey couldn't help but grin. "Surprise."

"Who . . ." Seht twisted hard to face Ravnos.

Ravnos let him turn around, but grabbed Seht's wrists, pinning Seht's hands above his head, the weapons splaying against the lift wall. He shoved a knee between Seht's legs and pressed inward. The unmistakable bulge of Seht's heavily aroused cocks pressed right up against his own erection. The raw pleasure forced a groan from his throat.

Seht didn't struggle, merely looked up at the taller and broader male. His gaze narrowed on Ravnos's face, clearly searching for something. "You can't be . . . But your scent . . ." His eyes widened and his lips parted. His spoke in the softest of whispers. "Aubrey?"

Ravnos smiled. "Long time, no see."

"Mother Night . . ." Seht lunged up on his toes to press his mouth against Ravnos's.

Ravnos parted his lips to engage Seht in an eager and ferocious biting kiss, teeth clicking against teeth, tongue battling tongue. This . . . *This* was what he'd been waiting for. He angled his head pressing Seht back against the wall, belly to belly, grinding his erection against Seht's. The rich musk of lust filled the tiny space.

Seht turned his head away, breaking the kiss and panting for breath. "I thought I was imagining it, your scent. I could only catch the smallest hint under the stink of humans."

Ravnos pressed his lips to Seht's exposed jawline and swept his tongue along it. "Comes from living among them."

Seht snorted and tugged his wrists. "Release my hands."

Ravnos grinned against Seht's throat. "But I kind of like you like this. I like the way you feel against me." He bit down lightly on the long muscle and massaged it with his tongue.

Seht groaned and lifted his chin, exposing the length of his throat to Ravnos's mouth. "I want to sheath my weapons."

Ravnos snorted and ground his erection against Seht's. "Is that what you're calling them these days?"

Seht groaned, then his lip curled in something close to a smile. "I was referring to my hands. They are going numb." He licked his lips. "I wish to touch you. I *need* to touch you."

The lift pinged, warning that the doors were about to open.

Sense splashed ice water through Ravnos's veins. *What the hell am I doing?* He released Seht and jumped back.

The Skeldhi prince lifted a silver brow and slid his sword and dagger into their respective sheaths with near-blinding speed. "Still shy?"

Ravnos kept a smile pasted to his lips. "Diplomatic courtesy."

Seht frowned.

The doors parted, revealing a man in a plain black visor dressed in a severely understated black frock coat and breeches tucked into flat black knee-high boots. His hands held no weapons with only a simple sword belted to his hip, but there was no mistaking the subtle scent of metal and hydraulic oils. The man was clearly a marine-class cyborg. Behind him stood six semi-armored men bearing electro-spears in dark blue fatigues emblazoned with the word, security across their chests.

The cyborg lifted his chin slightly. "Gentlemen."

Ravnos forcibly kept his expression nonchalant but winced inwardly. *Crap . . .* It hadn't even occurred to him to consider the security surveillance that had to have been in the lift. Fate only knew what kind of trouble he was in for his rather rash . . . conduct with the Skeldhi prince. He glanced over at Seht.

Seht met his glance and gave the smallest of smiles.

Ravnos stepped from the lift followed closely by Seht.

The six spearmen stepped past Ravnos and Seht to crowd into the lift followed by the cyborg.

Ravnos turned to stare in surprise. *I'm not under arrest?*

The cyborg grinned, winked, and the doors closed.

Seht snorted. "They are quite likely heading to the battle you just pulled me from or did you forget?" His lips tilted upward with the hint of a smile.

Ravnos stiffened. He *had* forgotten. He shot a glare at the amused prince.

Seht's brow lifted and his lips curved upward into a definite smirk. "How nice to know that you find me so . . . distracting." He took a step toward Ravnos.

Ravnos stepped back. Seht *was* distracting; too distracting. His worst nightmare had come true; he'd been discovered. Yet instead of fear, excitement was racing through him. Instead of considering ways to escape, his gloved hands clenched with the urge to grab Seht, find the nearest dark corner, and take him down to the floor so he could peel off all that gleaming black armor to get to the porcelain pale skin that was under it, and . . .

Seht lunged forward lightning quick, grabbing Ravnos's face with his hands. His mouth crashed onto Ravnos's and his tongue plunged past his parted lips.

CHAPTER NINETEEN

The flavor of Seht's kiss bloomed on Ravnos's tongue, triggering shudders of raw hunger. Practically devouring Seht's lips and tongue, Ravnos caught the Skeldhi prince around the waist and crushed him to his chest, lifting the slighter man from his feet. He teetered slightly off balance and crashed backwards into a wall. A quick twist and he was pressing Seht up against it, one knee jammed between the Skeldhi prince's thighs.

Using his tongue and teeth to answer Ravnos's kiss, Seht growled into Ravnos's mouth, a low and liquid rumble. His fingers slid from Ravnos's face to his shoulders, the long fingers digging in with bruising force. He turned his head sharply, breaking their kiss. "I can't feel a damned thing through this body armor."

Ravnos grinned. "Yours or mine?"

Seht snorted. "Both." The smile on his lips faded. "I searched everywhere for you."

Pain speared Ravnos through the heart. He released Seht and stepped back, forcing a smile onto his lips. "I was somewhat . . . preoccupied."

Seht's brow rose. "Apparently so . . . Captain." He nodded toward the silver braiding and the insignia on Ravnos's coat and smiled. "So, what do you fly?"

Ravnos smiled broadly and tugged on his lapels to set his coat back in place. "A very big ship." He nodded up the window-lined hallway before them and stepped toward it in silent enquiry.

Seht snorted. "A very big ship." He stepped alongside Ravnos, matching strides. "Why am I not surprised?"

Ravnos kept his gaze forward, his mouth shut, and the smile on his lips by force of will alone. Every ounce of pride urged him to tell Seht that he'd done well enough to have earned the captaincy of a demon-class dreadnaught, but he really had no interest in having his ship hounded all over known space by Skeldhi hunters.

Seht's brows rose. "You don't intend to tell me." It wasn't a question.

Ravnos's smile faded. "No."

Seht nodded. "Wise decision." His lips quirked into a sour smile. "You're not as rash as you used to be."

Ravnos winced and scratched the back of his head in embarrassment. "Oh sure, if you don't count charging into the middle of a battle to drag you into an elevator." *Stupid rehkyt instincts . . .*

Seht chuckled. "Well, some natural impulses are rather difficult to overcome."

Ravnos very nearly growled. "Fine, rub it in."

Seht tilted his head and a small smile appeared. "Don't mind if I do." His smile faded, and he folded his hands behind him. "You have no idea how glad I am that you chose to remain among the living." He closed his eyes briefly. "I could feel, in here . . ." He pressed a palm over his chest. "That you still existed." He turned to face Ravnos. "But it is not the same as having you before my eyes."

For one entire breath, Ravnos stared at the man who haunted his dreams, the one man that could destroy him, that *would* destroy him and everything he'd worked so hard to gain . . . and seriously considered letting him do just that. He forced his gaze away. *I can't give in like this. I won't!*

But he wanted to so badly his entire body ached with the urge.

Ravnos dropped his gaze to the floor before him. "I found

a reason to keep breathing." *Moribund's destruction . . .*

Seht's voice dropped to a soft whisper. "Syrhus told me that too much time had passed, that if you still lived, you would be entirely feral."

Feral? Ravnos snorted. "That's one way of putting it." *Especially when you consider my kill record of Moribund ships.*

At his back, Seht's hands tightened into fists. "He told me that if I found you, you would not come back to me willingly."

Pain stabbed straight through Ravnos's heart. He clenched his teeth, determined to ignore the savage ache from the gaping wound in his heart where his need for Seht continued to bleed. "Syrhus is right." He looked Seht square in the eye and tightened his jaw. "I'm not a scrawny kid in need of rescue anymore."

Seht snorted and shook his head. "No, scrawny is not how I would describe you at the moment."

Ravnos smiled. "That's nice to know." The tiniest hint of crushingly expensive cologne and designer hydraulic fluid drifted to Ravnos's nose. He stiffened, every hair on his body lifting in alarm. He took a deeper breath through his nose. The scent was unmistakable. Admiral Moraine, Moribund, was somewhere in the corridor ahead of them.

Seht's turned sharply to look at Ravnos. "What is it?"

Ravnos dropped his voice to a sub-vocal whisper. "Someone that does not need to see us together." He grabbed Seht by the arm and dragged him to the right, and the closest door. Reaching into the broad cuff of his coat sleeve, he pulled out a slender card and unwound the tiny wiretap. With the speed of long experience, he plugged the tap into the jack in the base of his skull, shoved the card into the door's reader, and slammed his personal lock-break code into the card.

Seht blinked then smiled, showing a hint of his long fangs. "An electronic lock-pick . . . Clever."

Ravnos flashed him a grin. "Merely practical."

The door clicked softly and slid to the right into the wall.

Before them was a darkened room filled with long rows of electronic file stations. A broad old-fashioned wooden desk occupied the back of the room under a tall window shielded from the sun by dark reflective blinds.

Ravnos's brow lifted. Apparently, they were in some sort of records room. He pressed Seht before him and into the room, then turned and hit the door panel just inside to close the door and lock it.

Seht strolled further into the room and looked about. "So who is it we are avoiding?"

Ravnos extracted the jack and rolled it up with the card. "Admiral Moraine of the Imperial fleet."

Seht turned to lean back against the desk and frowned at him. "So?"

Ravnos's jaw tightened and he spoke in a sub-vocal whisper. "Also known as Moribund."

Seht's eyes widened. "Blood and Night . . ."

The sound of multiple heavy footsteps carried through the door.

Ravnos stiffened. *What? Did he bring a small army or something?* Stepping as lightly as possible, he backed away from the door, moving deeper into the shadowed room. The back of his knees came in contact with the broad old-fashioned wooden desk.

Seht's hand closed on his shoulder.

Ravnos turned and eyed the prince. He didn't know what kind of detection equipment Moraine had with him, but the most basic of marine-class cyborg sensors could read how many people occupied a room that wasn't shielded against them. There was no way in hell that even the lowest ranking cyborg out there wouldn't detect them, which couldn't appear to be anything less than highly suspicious.

The corners of Seht's mouth lifted into a thoroughly lascivious smile. He took a step forward from the desk and pressed the ornate clasp of his fur-collared cloak. It opened under his fingers, letting the shimmering dark material fall to his ankles. He reached for the gleaming sword-belt around his hips and unbuckled it. The belt and sword joined the cloak on the floor. He grabbed the wrist clasps of his gauntlets, unfastened them, then yanked the gloves off, letting them fall to the pool of fabric at his feet.

Ravnos stared wide-eyed. To all intents and purposes, it looked as though Seht was getting undressed.

Seht winked and spoke on the sub-vocal level. "Clearly we are being spied upon. Shall we give them something worth observing?" He unfastened the shoulder clasps of his shimmering black body armor, letting the upper arm rerebraces and the attached lower arm vambraces fall away. He lifted his fingers to his neck and released the fastenings down the side of his chest armor one by one. The armor opened, revealing a skin-tight semitransparent shirt of iridescent black that did nothing to hide the rippling muscles beneath it. He pealed his chest armor away and dropped it. The musky perfume of raw lust rolled from his body.

The sight and scent went straight to Ravnos's already straining groin. He tugged his sword-belt open, practically throwing it from him, yanked off his belt sash, and jerked at his coat buttons, ripping a few off in his haste. His armored coat dropped to the floor with a heavy thump. He yanked at the bow on his cravat, practically shredding the material from his throat. His didn't bother to unbutton his waistcoat; he ripped it apart, the silver buttons flying everywhere.

Seht grinned openly, baring his long fangs, and clawed the front of his shirt, shredding it apart to reveal moon pale skin over whipcord muscle.

Ravnos followed suit, ripping his silk shirt apart as well to bare his broad chest. He bared his teeth in a grin as well and threw the rags of silk that had once been a shirt on the floor.

Seht's brows rose. "My, you certainly have grown."

Ravnos snorted. "Good genes."

Seht's grin widened. "You're welcome."

Ravnos blinked. "Eh . . ." He'd been referring to his father. *Oh, wait . . .* Seht had donated his DNA when he'd made him *rehkyt*. He rolled his eyes. "Proud of yourself?"

Seht lunged forward to grab Ravnos's face. "Very." He pressed an open-mouthed kiss to his lips.

Ravnos's mind emptied of everything but the warm muscular body in his arms, pressing against his chest and belly, the smooth skin under his fingers, and the heated mouth attempting to devour him. The burning hunger that had always simmered within him and remained unsatisfied no matter how many lovers he'd taken ignited in a firestorm of virulent and violent lust. He grabbed Seht by the shoulders and slammed him backwards down on the desk.

Seht grunted but reached up with both hands to grab Ravnos's dark red braid and yanked, pulling Ravnos's mouth from his. Seht's eyes narrowed to electric blue slits. He bared his fangs and spoke in a soft but harsh whisper. "I should never have left you to suffer in isolation this long."

Ravnos stared. *What . . .*

Lightning quick, Seht sank his long teeth into the right side of Ravnos's throat. Holding Ravnos's head firmly in place, he pulled his teeth free and swiped his tongue across the jagged tears.

Ravnos gasped in pain. Seht's bite had not been gentle and his licking wasn't much of an improvement. Abruptly, his sensitivity to sound, scent, and sensation increased to painful intensity, as did his lust. His vision, however, began to haze over and his limbs began to tremble. *Shit, Seht's venom . . .*

Seht pulled back, licked his lips, and slid a hand across Ravnos's bare chest. "Magnificent . . ." He captured a nipple in his long nails and plucked.

Carnal fire scorched along the path of Seht's fingers and stabbed straight down into Ravnos's dick forcing a gasping moan from his lips. *I forgot . . . I forgot what his touch feels like . . .* His hips rolled, rubbing against Seht's crotch in blatant hunger.

Seht's hands slid down to the waistband of Ravnos's pants. "Yes, yes . . . I know . . ." He tugged the belt open and the buttons free, opening his pants, then shoved the garment down past Ravnos's hips. "I know what you need." He grasped Ravnos's rigid cock and fisted his hand tight around it.

Ravnos choked. Seht's powerful grip felt so good it burned. It felt too good. He could feel his thoughts disintegrating, along with his hard-won control over his more bestial *rehkyt* nature. *No! I will not give in!* He grabbed Seht's wrists and yanked them up over his head, pinning them to the desk, then lifted his knee to the desktop, jamming it between Seht's thighs.

Seht twisted hard, struggling against Ravnos's unforgiving grip. He bared his teeth and snarled. "Release me!"

Ravnos focused on the silver-haired prince beneath him. It wasn't easy to keep hold of him by any means. He could feel by the straining muscles and the near inaudible whine of hydraulic servos that Seht was fighting him with every ounce of strength he possessed. However, Ravnos had the advantage of height, weight, and augmentations designed specifically for his more than human body. He smiled. "No."

Seht stiffened. "What?"

Pinning both of Seht's wrists in one fist, Ravnos reached down to unfasten Seht's pants. "No, I'm not letting you go." He reached under Seht's ass to grab the back of his waistband. "I'm not about to let an opportunity like this pass me by." With one hard tug, he yanked Seht's pants past his butt to his thighs, forcing both of Seht's knees up. His paired cocks slid free and arched up over his muscular belly toward his navel.

Seht bared his teeth. "You cannot do this!"

"Oh?" Ravnos broadened his smile. "Then stop me."

"I will . . ." Seht kicked out with his foot, aiming his sharp heel spur for Ravnos's kidneys.

"Whoa . . ." Ravnos twisted and grabbed the ankle of his boot. "Nasty little weapon you've got there." He yanked, pulling the knee boot free from Seht's leg. "Calm down. I'm not going to hurt you."

Seht's eyes narrowed to ice blue slits. "I will *not* make the same vow." He snarled and kicked out with his other heel.

Ravnos caught the other boot and his temper sparked. "Bastard . . ." He yanked the boot off and shot a narrow-eyed glare at Seht. "What, do you *want* me to hurt you?"

"You are welcome to try." Seht grinned, baring both his upper and lower fangs. "I am Skeldhi. Pain is one and the same with pleasure!"

"Is that so?" Ravnos smiled sourly. *Damn, I knew I shouldn't have left my whip back on the ship.* He licked his lips. *So, I'll just have to get creative.* What did he have to work with? He only had one hand. The other was occupied with holding Seht's. "Hmm . . ." He reached down and tugged a slender, finger-width throwing blade from the seam in his right boot.

Seht snorted. "Am I supposed to feel threatened by something so terribly small?"

Ravnos grinned, wishing, not for the first time, that he hadn't filed down his fangs. "Let me teach you an old Terran saying. It's not what you have, but what you *do* with it." He twirled the tiny flat blade between his fingers and brought the point to the very tip of Seht's nipple.

Seht froze, wide-eyed.

CHAPTER TWENTY

Standing between Seht's spread thighs, Ravnos stared down at the man he held by the wrists, flat on his back on the smooth smoked-glass topped desk, his frost-white hair spilling over the far edge.

Seht's gaze was focused on the point of the slender blade only a breath away from the tip of his nipple.

A cool and invigorating wave of excitement and anticipation rushed through Ravnos's veins. All that muscular and pristine white skin was under his complete control. He could feel his grin widening even further. He lifted the blade a tiny amount. "Hold still. This is very sharp, and I'd rather not do any permanent damage."

Seht swallowed, but otherwise, didn't twitch a muscle.

Ravnos flicked the blade in a precise circle around the very edge of Seht's aureole, the puckered pink flesh that surrounded the nipple. A thin line of scarlet welled up but didn't drip. The cut had only been deep enough to draw a very small amount of blood, but then, that was all he needed. He leaned very close and dragged his tongue all the way around the small cut, liberally soaking it in saliva.

Quickly, he rose back up and flicked the blade around the same circle, cutting lines from within to without through the circle like rays, sketching a seeping sun around Seht's nipple. This was something he hadn't attempted with any of his human lovers. It was generally far too intense for them.

Quickly, he moved to the other nipple and sketched yet another weeping circle. Another lick and more ray lines were added. Ravnos then propped his elbow down by Seht's left side and rested his chin on his fist, idly jiggling the tiny blade. He smiled.

Seht sucked in a slow breath and began to tremble, his muscles moving involuntarily. Both of his cocks swelled to a stiffness that actually pulled them away from his belly. The shafts darkened, the veins visibly pulsing with blood. The crowns bloomed to an angry purple. Clear, viscous fluid seeped from both crowns. He spoke in a hoarse whisper. "Your venom . . ."

Ravnos's brows lifted slightly, and his smile remained broad. "Potent, isn't it?"

Seht's brow was dotted with perspiration, but his lips curved into a smile. "So, you've become something of a sadist."

Ravnos's eyes narrowed and his smile tightened. "I had to find a way to handle my . . . aggression. Erotic sadism, giving pain to those who derive sexual excitement from it, has proved quite effective."

Seht's eyes closed and he began to pant. His closed eyes tightened, and he spat out something harsh in a language Ravnos's internal translator couldn't decipher.

Ravnos lifted his head from his upraised fist. *I think he's about reached his limit.* Wearing a smile he knew damned well was completely smug he twirled the tiny knife in his fingers. "Shall I continue?" He leaned close to Seht's pointed ear and whispered. "Or would you rather cum now?" He reached down, extended his index finger, and tapped the weeping crown of Seht's upper cock, hard.

Seht's eyes flew open wide, his body arched up hard and he released a loud choking scream. Every muscle in his body flexed, etched in stark relief, straining against Ravnos's hold on his wrists.

Ravnos jerked upright, his brows lifting in surprise, but he didn't let go of Seht's wrists. *I didn't think he'd be that sensitive to my venom?*

Seht dropped back down onto the desk, gasping with his mouth wide open. Tears spilled from the corner of his closed eyes. His face, throat, and chest flushed to a deep pink. Tears of blood wept from the cuts around his nipples.

Ravnos leaned over him, frowning. The pulse in the prince's wrists under his palm was strong but very fast. Apparently, his blood-pressure was actually causing the shallow cuts on his chest to bleed. "Are you alright?"

Seht opened his eyes. The cat-slits were dilated open to nearly full circular width with only a slender band of blue encircling the dark pupil. His entire body trembled. He spoke in a whisper. "L-let me c-cum."

Ravnos's frown deepened. He did not like the way Seht's eyes had dilated so far open. "Seht?"

Seht turned to face him snarling, his mouth stretched wide to bare his fangs to their fullest extent. "Let me cum!"

Ravnos's exposed cock pulsed, causing a small amount of precum to dribble free. He gasped with the ache of being harder than he'd ever been. The gleam of gold from the band around his wrist caught his eye. Captain Sear's gift . . .

Ravnos used Seht's wrists to pull him to the edge of the desk. The Skeldhi prince's bare feet landed on the floor, his legs bound together by his own pants around his thighs. He then turned the prince around to face the table, grabbed a handful of all that long white hair at the base of his neck, and shoved him face down on the desk, hard.

Seht threw up his arms, keeping his face from colliding with the table. "What are you doing?"

Ravnos stared at the round, firm, snow-white butt bent over the desk. "Merely fulfilling your wish." The prince was just far enough away that his cocks were not pressed against the desk's unyielding surface. He licked his lips. *Perfect.* He released Seht's hair for only a split second, just long enough to release the gold band from his wrist.

Seht shoved up onto his hands and glared at Ravnos from over his shoulder. "What are you . . ." His eyes widened. "What is that?"

Ravnos grabbed Seht's hair and shoved him back down. "Not for you." He slid the ring over the head of his exposed cock to the very base. *Anchor thirteen.* His internal array broadcast the keyword throughout his nervous system. The ring shrank until it snugly encompassed his straining length at the perfect place to keep him from ejaculating until he was ready to do so.

Eyeing Ravnos from over his shoulder, Seht's eyes widened. "A cock-ring?"

Ravnos grinned. "Pity I don't have any lube on me." He turned to the side so that Seht could watch him as he licked his hand." Beyond spit that is." He reached down to smooth his wet hand along the swollen length of his cock, taking the time to smear the dribbling precum all over the crown.

Seht's sapphire blue eyes widened to show white all the way around. "You are not planning to . . ."

Ravnos pressed his cock up against Seht's smooth white ass and ground in. The friction felt heavenly. He groaned in sheer pleasure. "Oh, but I am." He fell over Seht's back and whispered. "I suggest you push out very hard." He reached down to grasp himself and slid his cock down the crack of Seht's ass until his cock pressed against the tiny pucker right above Seht's balls.

Seht pushed hard under Ravnos's chest and growled. "You cannot do this. A rehkyt does not mount his master!"

Ravnos leaned down and whispered in his ear. "But I have no master." He shoved, pressing the head of his cock against the tight opening between Seht's cheeks.

Seht gasped and tensed, clearly resisting the intrusion.

Ravnos felt the red haze of urgency closing in on him. *Blood or sex . . .* His voice deepened to a rumbling growl. "You know what resistance does to someone like me. I suggest you stop because I won't." He pushed harder, the pressure from the head of his cock spreading Seht's anus open through sheer force.

Seht moaned, his head dropping to the desktop, then arched under him. His body opened.

The head of Ravnos's cock cleared the tight ring of muscles and forged into the hot, smooth velvet fist of Seht's ass. Inch by snug hot inch, his length was swallowed. He moaned in carnal bliss. A supremely pleasurable but aching pulse in his balls warned him that the cock-ring had been a very good idea. His body was already trying to climax.

Under him, Seht released a deep and guttural groan. "You are a complete and utter bastard of the first degree."

Ravnos stopped, pulled back just a bit. "That's what they tell me." He thrust in hard, slamming all the way into Seht's heat as far as he could go. The enveloping heat wrapped around his dick tightened in gentle suction, as though urging him even deeper. He released a heartfelt groan, nearly overwhelmed by hot velvet bliss. The tightness from the cock-ring around the base of his dick delivered just enough of an ache to make the sensation even sweeter.

Seht hissed and released the tiniest of whimpers. "You didn't even use your fingers to stretch me first."

Ravnos leaned down to lap at the shell of Seht's ear. "I thought you said you could handle a little pain?" He reached under to pinch one of Seht's nipples and rolled his hips, grinding his cock within to force the body he'd impaled to make room for him. He felt the slightest of bumps catch on the upper edge of his cock's crown.

Seht gasped and bucked hard.

Ravnos's grin widened. "Liked that, eh?" Apparently, he'd

caught Seht's prostate. He ground against it, just to be sure.

Seht moaned and shuddered, then arched and rolled his ass in reply.

Ravnos felt the velvet heat enveloping him tremble around his. "Oh yeah, you definitely liked that."

Seht snarled and bucked under him. "Shut up and fuck me, you sadistic son of a bitch!"

Ravnos tightened his grip on Seht's hair, forcing his head back down to the desk. "Temper, temper . . ." He licked his lips and reach down with his free hand to clasp the hot, rigid, dripping length of Seht's upper and primary cock. "But since you asked so sweetly . . ." He pulled back and braced his feet to either side of Seht's. "Your wish is my command." He thrust, hard, then, again and again, simultaneously stroking Seht's primary cock in time with his thrusts.

Gasping and moaning, Seht reached up to grab hold of the far edge of the desk, pushed up on his toes, and shoved back to meet him, stroke for stroke.

The hot, tight velvet glove sliding along Ravnos's dick delivering the most exquisite sensations combined with the rich perfume of Seht's lust tinted with the aroma of his blood. What little sanity he had left, evaporated. He leaned down to grasp Seht's shoulder in his flat teeth and bit down.

Seht choked and stiffened, his eyes going wide, then shuddered violently, and shouted. "Ah! Fuck!"

Heated wetness spilled over Ravnos's hand and pumped onto the floor beneath the desk. Seht had cum, finally.

His urgency well beyond the breaking point, Ravnos projected the release command to his cock-ring. The gold ring loosened. Ravnos slammed into Seht as hard as he could, once, twice . . . His balls tightened and released. Ecstasy burned from the base of his spine all the way up to the back of his skull, then back down all the way to the tip of his cock where he pumped every last drop of himself deep into the heated grip of Seht's ass. He threw back his head and shouted in raw carnal victory.

Ravnos collapsed on top of Seht's pale sweating back.

Seht panted for breath under him. "This was not how I planned to conclude our first meeting."

Ravnos lifted his head. "Yeah, well . . ." He licked across the bloody furrows his flat teeth had made across Seht's shoulder. "Plans change." His breathing deepened, seeking the other man's intoxicating scent of freshly spent lust.

Seht groaned. "That was not amusing."

Ravnos rose from Seht's back and pulled his flaccid cock free. He couldn't help but stare at his cum seeping from Seht's wide open anus. It was the most incredibly erotic thing he'd ever seen. A shiver raced through him and his cock twitched. He wanted . . . more. He wanted to see Seht with that half-lidded flush of spent lust spread out on the sheets of his bed. He wanted . . .

Ravnos jerked back, averting his gaze. He wanted what could never be. He spotted an open door and realized he was looking at a small facility. Yanking his pants up around his hips, he strode for the facility on shaking legs. He hadn't let himself go like that in . . . years.

Seht rose up on one elbow, his long silver hair spilling over his arms, and looked over at Ravnos. "Where . . ."

Ravnos didn't look back. "Facility. I need to get you cleaned up." The room was small but equipped with a flushing toilet, a sink, and plenty of soft white nubby towels. He grabbed a pair of the towels, ran the hot water under the sink, and soaked them thoroughly. After wiping himself off with one, he carried the other towel over to Seht, who had turned around to lean back on his elbows against the desk. His long silver mane spilled from his bowed head down his heaving chest. The prince was clearly exhausted. He appeared to be contemplating his pants, which were still down around his thighs.

Ravnos knelt by his bare feet and began the process of cleaning him as gently as he could. "Did I hurt you?"

Seht snorted. "Only my pride." He sighed. "I underestimated how strongly isolation would have affected you."

Ravnos looked up at him frowning. "What?"

Seht reached down and slid his fingers along Ravnos's cheekbone. "This was my fault."

Ravnos flashed him a smile, more than a little confused. "What are you talking about?"

Seht leaned down to cup Ravnos's face in both hands. "I should have looked harder for you. I should have found you sooner. I should have never let you go."

Ravnos stared into Seht's cat-slitted blue gaze and for an entire breath, he sincerely wished that, too. What would the last ten years have been like if he'd spent them with Seht?

Wearing a collar.

He shook his head free of Seht's hands and looked down at the floor. "We can't change the past. We can only move forward." It was something Captain Melchior had told him repeatedly. He leaned down to swipe the towel across the floor, cleaning up the last of the mess they'd made.

"Aubrey . . ."

"What's done is done." He rose to his feet, holding the soiled towel. "And my name is Ravnos." He turned on his heel and headed for the facility to get rid of the towel.

Seht reached down and pulled up his pants. "I never stopped missing you."

The stab of pain in his heart froze Ravnos where he stood. *God . . .*

Seht's voice dropped to a whisper. "I never stopped . . . loving you."

Ravnos's was heart pounding so loud he could hear the blood rushing in his ears. His hand tightened around the towel, but he didn't turn around. "I . . . I know."

"I'm here to take you home."

The heart pumping in Ravnos's chest stuttered with crushing pain, but he lifted his head and spoke strongly and firmly. "I already have a home, a life, and responsibilities." Moribund had to be destroyed. "It's too late for . . . us."

"Too late . . ." Behind him, Seht loosed a vicious snarl. "Never! As long as my blood runs in your veins, you belong to me."

Ravnos turned to face him, teeth bared. "No, Seht." A low growl rumbled deep in his chest. "I will *never* be anyone's slave ever again! Not even yours."

Tall, pale, and elegant, despite the rags of dark cloth hanging from his arms, and the cum dripping down the interior of his thighs, Seht's blue gaze narrowed and his jaw clenched. "No matter how well you disguise yourself, you can never be anything other than what you are, a Skeldhi *rehkyt*."

Ravnos turned his back on the man he'd just finished fucking. "I know." He strode into the facility with the distinct feeling that his heart was being ripped apart from the inside. He threw the towel against the wall. *I'm an idiot! Going anywhere near him was a mistake! I should have just left him in that hallway.*

To die by the hand of that cyborg?

He heaved a pained sigh. No, he couldn't have left him there, not Seht. He ran the cold water and scrubbed his face. *Stupid fucking rehkyt instincts . . .* He grabbed a fresh towel to dry his face and hands. *So now what do I do?* The only thing he could do. He'd just have to find a way to get the prince to stop his pursuit of him. He just hoped to the powers that be, that it wouldn't take one of them dying. On that depressing note, he took a moment to take a piss, rewash his hands, then opened the door to leave the facility.

Holding a small bundle of black cloth in his hands, Seht brushed right past him to get into the small room. "My turn." He closed the door behind him.

Ravnos was completely unable to stop the smile tugging at

his lips. *Somebody was in a hurry.* His gaze fell on the clothes and bits of armor scattered all over the floor. Cold hard reality kicked him square in the gut. He needed to get out of there, fast.

Moving as fast as his augmented limbs would allow, he tossed on his waistcoat, completely ignoring the shreds of his once fine silk shirt and cravat and threw his coat on over it without bothering to button it. He scooped up his sword-belt with his left hand and headed for the door to the hallway as quickly and silently as possible.

A white blur on the edge of his vision was the only warning he had. Ravnos backstepped, pivoting to his right, and threw up his sheathed sword.

Blocked, Seht's fist missed Aubrey's temple by only a fraction of an inch. He jerked back his fist and bared his long white fangs. "You are not leaving this room without my collar, Aubrey." Lightning fast, he swung his left fist, aiming for Ravnos's head.

Panic blazed white-hot up the back of Ravnos's skull. He grabbed the descending fist with his right hand and slammed the hilt of his sheathed sword against the side of Seht's head.

Seht's eyes rolled up, and he slumped to the floor. A trickle of blood stained his white mane at the temple.

Ravnos gasped in shock. "Oh shit!" Was he dead? He hadn't meant to hit him that hard! He dropped to his knees and pressed two fingers to Seht's throat. A pulse throbbed under his fingers. *He's not dead.* Relief flooded through him, making his entire body tremble, but anger followed in its wake. "Damn it, Seht!" He rose to his feet, but indecision held him rooted to the spot for an entire heartbeat. He didn't like leaving him there on the floor where anyone could just walk in on him.

Unfortunately, he didn't have a choice. Seht clearly had no intention of taking 'no' for an answer. He needed to get out of there.

Ravnos opened the door just enough to see that the hallway was deserted. He slipped out the door into the hallway, closed the door behind him, and locked it. He took an extra second to use his wiretap to scramble the code so that the lock would refuse to open from the inside. He smiled grimly. *You're not getting out of there any time soon, you stubborn shit.* He headed up the hall at a quick march away from the Skeldhi prince. Lifting a finger, he activated the com-unit still clinging to his ear. "*Imp one,* this is the captain."

Ravnos's ear com crackled to life. "We read you, Captain. Status?"

"Status, code blue." *Evacuation, all personnel.* He needed to get out of there while he still had a few shreds of sense left. "On my mark, execute." *Track me and collect.*

Behind a certain closed door, Seht's voice lashed out in an angry shout. "Aubrey, you bastard! I will hunt you to the ends of the universe to set my *shen* on your throat! You *will* be claimed, and you *will* bow to your master if it takes the rest of my life!"

Ravnos bolted. "Pick the closest exit, and don't bother being polite!"

Twenty steps ahead of him, a window exploded, scattering smoke and shards of glass all over the hallway.

A dark-coated man draped in veils of smoke stepped through the window, his boots crunching on shattered glass. "Your egress is ready, Captain."

CHAPTER TWENTY-ONE

Twenty minutes later, Ravnos's entire crew was back on the small sleek captain's gig and heading out into space, straight for their ship.

Seated in his chair by the window, still in his battered coat, torn waistcoat, and shirtless, Ravnos set the communications headset down with a sigh. President Kidd had been somewhat understanding. The cyborg attack had completely ruined his dinner plans to show off his new captain to several of his more choice senators and council members, so he'd understood why Ravnos hadn't shown up. He'd even understood the necessity of losing a hallway window on the five-hundredth and sixth floor of his tower for an emergency escape from Admiral Moraine.

Ravnos hadn't even flinched when he'd told that lie.

However, the president had been less than understanding about Ravnos feeling the need to leave for his ship. The headset crackled softly. "There's something you are not telling me, isn't there, Captain Ravnos?"

Ravnos had taken a breath then sighed. "Yes, Mr. President, there is."

Silence had crackled across the line. "Is it . . . a personal matter?"

Ravnos looked over at his worried lieutenant, hovering in the doorway to the crew's area. "Yes, Mr. President."

The president heaved a sigh so heavy it came across the headset loud and clear. "Fine. I might as well send you on a hunting mission. There are a couple of unidentified small ships sitting a little too close to our borders in the eighth quadrant. Get them to identify themselves. Use as much force as you deem necessary."

Ravnos couldn't help but smile. "Thank you, Mr. President."

"However, as soon as your personal matter is resolved, I expect you back here and ready to go to every single dinner engagement I care to send you to!"

Ravnos winced. "Yes, Mr. President."

The president cleared his throat. "Excellent. Good hunting, Captain."

"Thank you, Mr. President." The sound of empty air crackled across the headset. Ravnos removed it and handed it to his lieutenant. "Tell the *Hellsbreath's* nav-pilot that we need to be ready to leave for the eighth quadrant as soon as we arrive."

The lieutenant's eyes widened. "The eighth quadrant, sir?"

Ravnos rolled his eyes. "Don't worry, you'll get your shore leave as soon as we get back." He looked out the window at the world fading in the distance. "I just have something . . . personal to take care of, first."

The lieutenant snapped his hand up to his brow in a salute. "Understood, Captain." He lowered his hand. "I'll have your day uniform ready for you in five minutes."

Ravnos lifted his brow at the man.

The lieutenant scowled at him. "The ship's crew does not need to see you in . . ." He waved his hand indicating his captain's clothes. " . . . *This* condition."

Ravnos rolled his eyes. "I *so* need to get you a first officer."

The lieutenant smiled brightly. "Make sure you pick a good one."

Ravnos gave him a sour smile. "I intend to." He turned stare out the window at the stars. He strongly suspected that he was being sent to deal with some Moribund ships, seeing as Moribund was in the neighborhood. However, for some reason, he simply couldn't find the enthusiasm he normally felt at such occasions. He rubbed the heel of his hand across the center of his chest over an ache that seemed to center around his heart.

The alarm bell sounded, and the ship's intercom buzzed to life. "Captain, we are being pursued."

Ravnos froze. *What?* His heart slammed in his chest double-time. *Seht couldn't have followed me this fast . . .* He hit the intercom button built into his chair. "What kind of craft?"

"It appears to be . . . Skeldhi, a small one." The man cleared his throat. "About the size of this gig, sir."

Ravnos's nails dug into the arm of his chair. It *was* Seht, he'd bet his sword on it. The small hairs on his neck rose and a cool sweat spread across his shoulders. *Stubborn bastard . . .* He almost smiled. "How far behind are they?"

"About twenty minutes and gaining."

Ravnos's gaze narrowed. *Looks like I'll have to prepare a welcome.* "Can you tell how many are on the ship?"

"According to our sensors . . . one, sir."

Ravnos blinked. That had to have been wrong. "One? Are you sure?"

Silence buzzed across the intercom. "Confirmed. Only one occupant sir, and they appear to be flying their craft mechanically. No nav-pilot."

Anger flashed up the back of Ravnos's skull. *That suicidal idiot!* He fisted his hand on his chair. *What is he thinking, flying alone into unknown territory?* His lips pulled back from his teeth. *He needs to be taught a lesson.* "Can we outrun them?"

The man snorted. "Easily, sir."

Ravnos took a deep breath and smiled. "Good, don't."

"Don't?"

Ravnos tapped his fingers on the arm of his chair. "Correct. Don't outrun them. Stay just out of weapon's range and lead them straight to the ship. Communicate to the *Hellsbreath*, use the electromagnet to capture the ship and pull it into an unused hanger. Once there, seal it from entry or exit."

"Shall we leave it in vacuum, sir?"

"No. Full atmosphere and gravity at human temperature." Ravnos smiled even as a low growl rumbled deep in his chest. That foolish Skeldhi prince would finally learn whom he was truly dealing with. "No one goes in or out of that dock but me, understood?"

"Yes, s-sir! R-right away, sir!"

Ravnos blinked. Had the man just stuttered?

A voice spoke softly at Ravnos's side. "You really shouldn't growl at the staff, sir."

Ravnos turned to find his lieutenant at his elbow, his hands filled with his fresh uniform.

The lieutenant stood perfectly straight, his blue gaze, perfectly steady, but there was a fine sheen of sweat on his upper lip. "Believe me, you're already intimidating enough."

Ravnos snorted. "Is that so?"

The lieutenant grinned. "It's a good thing they don't see you when you haven't yet had your morning coffee."

Ravnos rolled his eyes. He waved at the clothes in his lieutenant's hands. "Never mind those, they'll only be destroyed."

"Eh?" The lieutenant flinched back, cradling the uniform protectively in his hands. "Destroyed . . ."

Ravnos stood up to shrug out of his coat and vest. "Take this, too." He handed the only slightly rumpled vest to his lieutenant. "It should still be salvageable." He strapped his sword-belt around his hips and slid the coat back on without bothering to button it over his bare chest. "Have a fresh uniform and coat ready for me once I deal with our uninvited guest." He sat back down.

"Deal with . . ." The lieutenant's eyes widened. "By

yourself, sir?"

Ravnos turned and narrowed his gaze on him. "You wouldn't be implying that I am incapable of handling one man, would you?"

The lieutenant stiffened and swallowed visibly. "N-no, sir. Not at all, sir!"

"Excellent." Ravnos smiled tightly. "You're dismissed, lieutenant."

"Yes, sir." The lieutenant lifted his hand to his brow in a smart salute, turned on his heel, and strode from the captain's cabin with dignified haste.

Ravnos departed the gig, stroke calmly across the deck of the shuttle bay, and entered the lift. Once he stepped free of the lift and into the long steel-line hallway, he broke into a flat-out run through corridor after corridor. His open coat winged out behind him.

At the edges of his mind, the ship's consciousness murmured a welcome to her captain, but her focus was elsewhere. She was very busy with the task of bringing a difficult and unruly spacecraft safely into its assigned hanger bay. However, she took it upon herself to open the doors to corridors empty of personnel while locking others to keep people out just long enough to allow her captain the freedom go where he pleased in perfect privacy.

An agonizing number of minutes later, Ravnos arrived at the huge round pressure door that marked the entry to the hanger bay in question. He stared up at the blank steel surface shaking with the urge to throw the door open and dreading the purpose behind doing so.

Seht was on the other side of that door.

His blood surged with a near-violent craving to see the silver-haired Skeldhi prince once more. At the same time, the cold sweat of despair slid along the base of his spine with what he would have to do once he had. Somehow, he had to convince the prince to go back and never pursue him again. He could not afford to let Seht stand in the way of his mission to destroy Moribund. Every day that monster remained breathing, people and ships would die for no reason other than profit.

He closed his eyes and bowed his head. *Please . . . Don't make me kill you.* He took a deep breath, raised his head, and asked the ship to open the door.

The bay was empty but for a single sleek and elegant craft of unrelieved highly reflective silver with back-swept wings for atmospheric flight. It crouched on four legs in the very center of the expansive empty bay, steaming and dripping from the ice melting on its hull. On its side, a door spiraled open and a staircase oozed into being.

Ravnos took a deep breath and drew his live-steel sword and the parrying dagger from behind him.

Seht stepped from his craft bare-chested in only his trousers and boots with a sword in his hand. His long white mane had been pulled back into a snug tail. He bared his teeth and loosed a liquid snarl. "Ravnos . . ."

Ravnos lifted his chin. "*Captain* Ravnos of the demon-class dreadnaught *Hellsbreath*, chartered with the Republic of the Caribbean Stars. I do not wish to start a war with the Skeldhi. Please return to your ship and go."

Seht stared at Ravnos with his eyes narrowed and his jaw tight. "I am not leaving without you." He twitched his off-hand and uncoiled a whip.

Ravnos slid one foot back, angling his body into a casual fighting stance, his weapons held loosely in his hands. "Yes, you are." Something from the depth of his memory suddenly surfaced. "I deny your claim to me."

Seht's eyes widened and his body stiffened as though struck.

Ravnos kept himself from wincing, but it wasn't easy. *Damn, he looks like he's about to cry.*

Abruptly, Seht's chin lifted, his gaze narrowed, and he bared his teeth. "Then I will *make* you accept my claim." He lifted his blade and lunged his blade pointed at Ravnos's heart.

Cool excitement raced up Ravnos's spine. *That's what you think.* He intercepted Seht's blade on the flat of his, forcing Seht's blade off target, and lunged in to meet him hilt to hilt. He smiled from only a kiss away. "I am not an un-augmented child this time."

Seht grinned, showing his fangs. "So I see." He shoved hard and twisted, breaking contact with Ravnos's sword. He lashed out with his whip, aiming low.

Ravnos spotted the whip and leaped straight up, avoiding the lash. His augmented legs lifted him high off the deck.

Seht leaped upward matching his height and swung for Ravnos's upper arm.

In mid-air, Ravnos swung out his forearm-length parrying dagger hard, caught Seht's blade and used the momentum created by the hit to twist all the way around. His sword whipped out and scored a slice across Seht's upper sword arm.

Seht curled his lip in a hiss but didn't drop his blade. He slammed the heel of his whip-hand into Ravnos's chest, shoving him away. He landed on the floor in a crouch. Scarlet dripped on the steel deck.

Ravnos landed in a crouch two body-lengths away.

Seht snarled and charged him.

Ravnos growled low and deep and ran to meet him.

Lightning fast, live-steel met live-steel in thrust and counterthrust parry and spark-inducing slide. The bay echoed with the tang of ringing steel from strike after strike, punctuated by the occasional whip-crack. Scarlet splotches spattered across the steel decking.

Annoyed at the difficulty he was having getting his sword past Seht's defense, Ravnos twisted to avoid a stab, his coat flaring out, and lashed out with a hard kick. It landed solidly on Seht's left side.

Seht gasped but countered with a whip-hand punch aimed for Ravnos's head.

Ravnos jerked back, but still felt a glancing slam to the edge of his jaw. He twisted away and added a long backwards flip hard enough and high enough that his hands didn't need to touch the deck. He landed in a crouch, his coat pooling around him on the deck plates.

Two body-lengths away, Seht crouched, panting for breath. He frowned. "That fighting style . . . Where did you learn it?"

Ravnos stood up and spat a small amount of blood. He rubbed his jaw with the heel of his sword hand. "From a cousin." He couldn't help the smile lifting his lips. "A very *distant* cousin."

Seht snorted. "Ah, an *isfeht*, a renegade *rehkyt*."

Ravnos shrugged slightly. "Well, he did have red hair."

Seht's brow lifted. "And fangs no doubt. No human is capable of fighting in that fashion. Even with augmentations, their spatial sense wouldn't allow for it."

Ravnos shrugged again but noted the small rents in Seht's ship-suit all along his arms and upper thighs. He wasn't much better. His coat and trousers had almost as many slashes. Scarlet was dotting the plates under both of them. He'd been careful to avoid cutting the arteries under Seht's neck, arms, or along the inner thighs. He didn't want to kill him if he could avoid it.

Ravnos did a quick survey of his own wounds and noticed exactly the same pattern of slices along his arms and outer thighs. Seht wasn't trying to kill him either. However, with as much blood-loss as they'd already suffered, came disorientation. He had to stop the fight before one of them accidentally did something fatal.

It was time to fight dirty. He tossed his parrying dagger across the bay. He'd need his hands for this.

Seht lifted his chin and snorted, a smile curving his lips. "If you think I'll toss my whip aside, you are sorely mistaken."

Ravnos licked his lips and smiled. *Good.* He twirled the sword in his hand. "Not feeling honorable?"

Seht's smile evaporated. "Fuck honor." He flicked his wrist, making his whip coil at his heels. "I will use *any* means to get you back!" He lunged toward Ravnos and lashed out with his whip.

Ravnos reached out with his off-hand and allowed the whip to wrap around his wrist. It stung like a bitch. Wincing only slightly, he grabbed the wire-laced leather, side-stepped, and yanked hard, throwing his entire weight to the side.

Seht was thrown in the opposite direction, skidding on his heels in an arc.

Ravnos crouched lower and continued his hard turn, making it more of a spin. Just before Seht could completely lose his balance, he pulled hard and lunged toward Seht, using the tension from the whip for greater speed. At the very last moment, he tossed his sword away and threw his right arm out to catch Seht around the neck.

Seht's eyes widened, then he fell back under Ravnos's weight.

With Seht's off-hand caught under his body, Ravnos grabbed his own wrist, putting Seht into a headlock.

Seht released the whip to grab at Ravnos's hair. "Let go!" He brought up his sword, aiming the pommel for Ravnos's head.

Ravnos winced and hissed from the pain of his hair being yanked, but only loosened his hold on Seht's throat enough to roll onto his back and halfway under Seht to avoid the descending pommel. He tightened his hold around Seht's throat once more and yanked Seht squarely on top of him. "No."

Seht choked, grabbed for Ravnos's arm, and rolled hard to the side.

Ravnos spread his legs wide to keep himself under the silver-haired prince. He growled in Seht's pointed ear. "Pulling hair? I thought only girls fought that way."

Gasping, Seht kicked out and struggled to sit upright. "Bastard!" His sword clanged on the steel deck.

Ravnos decided to help him sit up and rolled forward. With a hasty bit of wiggling, he got both knees bent under him, and safely away from Seht's sword. He angled his choking-hold arm high, aiming to stop the blood flow in the arteries on the sides of Seht's neck to make Seht pass out as quickly as possible.

Seht's struggles weakened, his sword dropped to the floor with a clang.

Ravnos pressed his cheek against Seht's. "I have no desire to kill you, Seht. You're free to go. I just wanted to prove to you—to both of us, that you can't dominate me. It's far too late for that. I will never go back with you."

Seht sucked in a harsh breath. "If you will not come with me . . ." He gasped in another breath. "Then, I will not leave."

"What?" Ravnos stiffened. "Are you insane?"

Seht wheezed in another breath. "I will not . . . leave you . . . again."

A strange dizziness filled Ravnos's brain. "You're willing to stay with me here, under my command?"

Seht gasped. "Yes."

Ravnos growled in his ear. "You are absolutely sure?"

Seht sucked in a deep breath and his eyes closed. "I am . . . sure. I will *not* leave you again. I . . . I can not live without you . . . anymore." A tear slid from his eye and his voice faded. "I tried. I can not . . . I will not . . . anymore. You are . . . my other . . . half." His body went limp in Ravnos's arms.

In complete shock, Ravnos released the silver-haired prince's throat and let him fall back into the cradle of his arms. He closed his eyes against the searing ache in his heart and in his throat. Wetness burned down his cheeks. *Blood and hell . . . Seht wanted to be with him badly enough to stay?* He opened his eyes to look blearily up at the distant struts of the bay unable to tell if he was thrilled or horrified. He looked over toward the bay door and smacked his forehead. "Fuck . . . What do I *do* with him?"

CHAPTER TWENTY-TWO

Tired, sweating, and bleeding from a hundred shallow cuts all over him, Ravnos marched through the passageways clasping the legs of the unconscious and bleeding Skeldhi prince he'd flung over his shoulder.

His lieutenant met him at the door to the captain's suite and blinked. "I know I asked you to get us a first officer, Captain, but . . ." He pulled open the captain's door and gave his captain a weak smile. "You really didn't need to go so far as to kidnap one, sir."

Ravnos stopped in the doorway and blinked. *First officer* . . . He eyed the unconscious prince and a slow smile lifted his lips. *Perfect.* He turned back to his lieutenant and his smile broadened. "I believe the old naval term is 'pressed,' as in, 'press-ganged.'"

His lieutenant's eyes widened. "Uh . . . Why so it is, sir."

Ravnos lifted his chin. "I'll need a full set of uniforms, for both of us."

The lieutenant followed at his captain's heels. "Captain, you mean he really *is* going to be our first officer?"

Ravnos lifted one brow. "Do you have any objections as to how I acquire my officers, lieutenant?"

The lieutenant hastily shook his head and lifted both hands. "Oh, no, sir! Not at all, sir! But, um . . ." He eyed the both of them, then looked pointedly at the carpet under Ravnos's boots. "Shall I get someone from medical down here, first?"

Ravnos stared down at the blood dripping onto his carpet.

"Hmm . . . Perhaps you should." He strode past his neatly made four poster bed, heading for the bathing facility and called over his shoulder. "Oh, and ask security to bring up a full set of force cuffs, ankles, and wrists."

The lieutenant tripped on nothing in particular. "Force cuffs, sir?"

Ravnos opened the door to his private facility. "Your new first officer has a nasty temper." He set the unconscious prince on the tile floor and pulled out one of his slender boot-knives.

"Yes, sir! Right away, sir!" The lieutenant turned on his heel to face away from the facility door. He tapped his ear-jack. "Medical, please. Thank you. Medical? I need a first aid medical team in the captain's quarters, on the double. Yes, first aid only. Good. Thank you."

Ravnos yanked off Seht's boots and began cutting Seht's blood-stained clothes from his body.

"Acquisitions, please? Yes, I need a full set of uniforms for a first officer. Size? Um . . ."

Ravnos focused on the ship's sentience.

It only took a split second for the ship to assure her captain that she had indeed made a full scan of the Skeldhi prince, including clothing size.

"The ship has his measurements on file." Ravnos threw the torn and bloody fabric against the wall with a wet splat. "Look under Deshryt, Seht." *Prince Seht . . .*

The lieutenant nodded. "The ship has the required measurements filed under Deshryt Seht. Yes? Good. Thank you. Security please."

Ravnos rose to soak a towel in the small sink then went back to Seht to wipe off some of the blood.

"Security? The captain requires a full set of force cuffs, if you please. Yes. Ankles and wrists. Immediately." The lieutenant tapped his toe. "No, this is *not* a fucking joke!"

Ravnos turned toward the facility door. "Security! Get me

a goddamned set of force cuffs right the fuck now! That's an order!"

The lieutenant snorted. "Any more questions? No? Good. Thank you."

The door chime sounded.

The lieutenant hurried to the door and admitted the medical team.

Patched, cleaned, dressed, and groomed within an inch of his life, Ravnos strode into his ready room. He swept a hand through his shoulder-length red waves then down the cuffed sleeve of his freshly pressed and cleaned captain's coat. He took a moment to ask the ship for the current duty roster, then folded his arms, and leaned back against his desk eying the frost-haired prince slumped over in the heavy-duty security chair. He had no doubts about the chair holding Seht firmly. It was designed to hold a marine-class cyborg.

It had taken two of his lieutenant's two yeomen to dress the unconscious prince. The force cuffs around Seht's ankles and wrists were tuned into the prince's augmentations, so despite the fact that Seht had been unconscious, the verbal command to stand had been more than enough to keep him upright.

The yeomen had done an impressive job.

Seht's long silver mane had been combed back from his brow and tied at the base of his neck with a blue bow that would match the prince's eyes perfectly. His pale cream silk shirt was impeccably tied at the neck with a starched lace-trimmed cravat. A neatly pressed brocaded black waistcoat fell to his knees over snug black seamed trews. The silver braided, black velvet long coat was buttoned to the heart and tied with a broad blue sash that matched the ribbon in his hair. They'd even found gleaming black knee boots that fit over his ankle cuffs.

Ravnos's brow lifted. *Damn. He looks good in that.* The white bandages down his arms and legs didn't even show.

All that was left was to wait until Seht awakened and presented him with an offer he couldn't refuse. According to the ship's mind, that would be happening any second . . .

Seht groaned, winced, and struggled to sit up in the chair. He stared at his cuffed wrists and his eyes widened. "What . . ."

Ravnos drew his sword. It was time to induct his brand new first officer. He glared down at his captive. "I offer you the position of first officer on my ship, the *Hellsbreath*. Do you accept?"

Seht's hands fisted in the cuffs attached to the arms of the chair but his eyes widened. "First Officer . . . You wish me as second in command?"

Ravnos nodded. "You will obey no one's orders but mine, but mine you will obey without question. Do you accept?"

Seht's gaze narrowed. "This is your condition to remain?"

Ravnos held Seht's gaze steadily, despite the fact that his heart was beating in his throat. "You may leave any time you wish."

Seht curled his lip, showing a long fang. "But if I . . . serve as your first officer, I may remain?"

Ravnos nodded. "Yes."

Seht lifted his chin. "I accept."

"Very well then . . ." Ravnos knelt at Seht's side to release his wrists then stepped away. "Kneel and make your oath."

Seht rubbed his wrists and stood. He dropped to one knee and placed one hand flat on the deck. The black skirts of his coat flared around him. He looked up at Ravnos.

Ravnos set the edged tip of his sword against Seht's bare throat. He smiled. "Swear."

"I, Deshryt Seht, solemnly swear on my honor to serve . . ." He curled his lip. "Captain Aubrey Laslo Ravnos of the mercenary ship *Hellsbreath* . . ."

Ravnos barely held onto his smile. He hadn't realized that Seht knew his full name.

" . . . with all due honor, loyalty, and respect."

Ravnos's smile widened to a grin. "And obedience."

Seht clenched his teeth.

Ravnos raised his brow in an open dare to omit his addition. He pressed the blade a little more firmly to Seht's throat. A trickle of blood dribbled down to stain Seht's cravat.

Seht's gaze narrowed. "And obedience, until death . . ." He flashed a smile. "Or his capture by Skeldhi hunters."

Ravnos let the growl in his chest surface. "You were supposed to say, or until I remove you from duty."

Seht let the smile fade from his lips. "You will have to kill me to remove me from your side. I will not be dismissed. As for the other . . ." His gaze narrowed. "The hunters still have you on their list. Sooner or later, they will find you. You can only outrun your fate for so long."

Ravnos curled his lip in a very nasty smile. "I've done pretty well so far."

Seht smiled just as nastily. "Why, so you have." He cleared his throat. "By the grace of Mother Night and the glory of my queen, may I serve with distinction."

"I accept." Ravnos removed the blade from Seht's throat and stepped away. "Blood and Night, you're a stubborn bastard."

Seht stayed down on his knee but lifted one silver brow. "To quote one of your Terran sayings, it takes one to know one."

"Why so it does." Ravnos tugged a handkerchief from his coat sleeve and wiped the tip of his blade. The white fabric came away stained with red. "You may rise."

Seht rose to his feet. "Thank you . . . Captain." He lifted both hands, letting the lace fall back, revealing the gold titanium cuffs on his wrists. "And these?"

Ravnos narrowed his eyes at Seht and smiled. "I didn't have a collar."

Seht's eyes narrowed and his jaw tightened. "I see." He lowered his hands and carefully drew the draping lace down over the gleaming cuffs around his wrists. "So, now what?"

Ravnos sheathed his blade. "Now, we go to an officers meeting where we discuss the destruction of the Moribund ships in the eighth quadrant."

Seht nodded and smiled. "I like the sound of that."

Ravnos's smile turned feral. "Afterwards, I take you to my personal quarters, where I introduce you to my desk."

Seht's brow lifted. "Another desk?"

Ravnos reached for his coat and slid into it. "Actually, it's the same one." He turned to smile at Seht. "President Kidd had it delivered, as a . . . gift in congratulations for taking a first officer."

Seht frowned. "You told him?"

Ravnos shrugged. "I sent him an update of the ship's crew log."

Seht winced. "He must have seen the security tape . . ."

Ravnos smiled. "That, too." He turned and walked to the door. "This way, if you please."

Seht followed at his left heel.

Ravnos led his new first officer through the smoked steel passageways of his ship, introducing him to the key members of his crew from the bowel-deep engineering corps all the way up to the dour nav-pilot and his four sub-pilots on the bridge.

Seht folded his hands behind him and asked polite but pointed and knowledgeable questions about everything from the ship's functions and distribution of duties to astro-mechanics and protocol.

Despite the fact that Seht was clearly not human, the crew appeared to respond quite favorably to their charming first officer, using tones of respect when addressing him.

Ravnos barely noticed. He was too busy absorbing the way Seht's hair shimmered frost-white against the black velvet of his coat, and the way the cream silk of his collar and cravat warmed his porcelain pale skin. He found himself distracted by the way Seht strode with grace and balance, gliding lightly on his feet despite the extra weight of his mechanical augmentations. When he spoke, his voice held almost a bell-tone. The subtle erotic musk of his scent perfumed the air around him. *He's so damned . . . beautiful.*

And exciting . . .

His blood began to race until it pounded deep and low, tightening his trousers. Every smile and gesture became a reminder of the way Seht's tight hot body had moved under him, and around him . . . the sounds of flesh striking flesh, the scent of blood, and semen . . .

By the end of the tour, Ravnos led Seht into his private office practically breathless with lust.

His lieutenant spoke softly at his shoulder. "Excellent choice for first officer, Captain." His voice held profound satisfaction.

Ravnos started. He'd completely forgotten that he'd asked the lieutenant to meet him at his private office.

The lieutenant stepped past his captain, winked, then turned on his heel to face him holding a large red leather-bound book. A black ribbon marker trailed from the pages.

Seht turned and lifted his brow at the lieutenant. "I'm glad you approve."

Ravnos bit back a smile. Seht had *very* sharp hearing.

The lieutenant's eyes widened, and his cheeks flushed. He ducked his head, dodging Seht's sharp blue gaze, and cleared his throat. With a respectful bow, he pulled an antique-styled ink pen from his breast pocket and held out the book. "As you requested, Captain."

Ravnos took the book and the pen from his hands. "Thank

you." He turned to set the book on his desk and opened it to the creamy white page marked by the ribbon. He turned to Seht and pointed at the open page. "Sign your name here."

Seht frowned at the list of names on the page. "What exactly am I signing?"

Ravnos folded his arms across his chest. "Crew's log."

Seht lifted a brow at Ravnos. "An actual book? How . . . archaic." He took the pen from Ravnos and turned to sign his name and the title of first officer in neat Terran script.

"I prefer to see it as traditional." Ravnos felt his lieutenant slip something heavy into his coat pocket. *Ah yes, my . . . gift.* Anticipation spilled through him, but he held back the shit-eating grin that wanted to burst forth.

Sent finished his signature and set the pen beside the book.

Ravnos closed the book and collected the pen. He turned and handed both to his lieutenant. "Is everything prepared?"

The lieutenant saluted. "As requested, Captain."

Ravnos lifted his chin and smiled. "We will be there momentarily."

The lieutenant nodded. "Yes, sir." He strode across the stateroom and left, closing the door behind him.

Seht stared after the lieutenant, then turned back to Ravnos. "The officer's meeting?"

Ravnos looked away and tugged the gloves from his hands. "Yes." He unbuckled his sword-belt and set it to lean against the side of his desk. "But before that appointment . . ." He tugged the buttons of his coat open. "I have a personal gift for you." He smiled.

Seht took a wary step back, his eyes narrowing. "Is that so?"

Ravnos reached into his left pocket and pulled out a palm-sized golden ring a finger's width in thickness and held it up so that the rainbow sheen of nanites was clearly visible.

Sent frowned. "A mimetic ring?"

Ravnos grinned. "A mimetic *cock*-ring, to be precise."

Seht's eyes widened.

Ravnos narrowed his eyes at Seht. "Your hands and elbows on my desk. Now."

Seht's hands trembled then jerked back, yanking his body backwards. They slammed palm down onto the desk followed by his elbows, forcing Seht to arch back partway over the desk. He winced, then bared his teeth in a snarl. "What in the name of Night are you doing?"

Ravnos stepped close and jerked open the sash around his coat. With blindingly fast movements, he unfastened the coat buttons, then the waistcoat buttons. "What am I doing?" Ravnos paused to give Seht a narrow-eyed smile. "Why, I thought that'd be obvious." He undid the zipper fly to Seht's pants and jerked his trews down to his knees. "I'm giving you your gift." He took Seht's primary cock into his hand and stroked.

Seht groaned.

The smooth, warm flesh in Ravnos's hand twitched and hardened. He slid the ring onto Seht's cock and pushed it all the way to his balls. He opened his mouth and released a stream of electronic white noise, the locking code.

Seht winced, clearly not liking the sound.

The ring closed snugly around Seht's erect flesh.

Seht choked, then narrowed his eyes at Ravnos. "Cock-ring indeed. I am guessing that the hideous sound you just uttered is some sort of activation code?"

Ravnos flashed him a grin. "Good guess." He looked back down, admiring the gleaming ring and the pink and ivory flesh it contained. "Very nice." He released him, then leaned over him, placing his own hands on the desk, framing Seht's body. "Gold suits you."

Seht hissed in a breath. "It's . . . tingling."

Ravnos nodded solemnly. "It does that." The microscopic

machines, the nanites, not only shaped the ring for a perfect and snug fit, they also vibrated the flesh just enough to keep the wearer's attention firmly focused.

His wrists and arms pinned to Ravnos's desk by his own augmentations, Seht writhed a small amount. "I had no idea you had a sadistic streak."

Ravnos snorted. "It's something I acquired." His voice was very dry. His hands moved in a blur to fasten up Seht's clothes.

Seht curled his lip. "You're going to leave me like this?"

Ravnos smiled. "We have a meeting to go to." He stepped back. "You are free to stand, but you may not touch yourself or remove the ring."

Seht straightened. "How long?"

Ravnos lifted his brows. "This meeting includes dinner, so I'd say about three hours."

Seht's mouth fell open. "You're leaving me in this cock-ring for *three hours*?"

Ravnos's smile curled to show his teeth, and once again found himself regretting that he hadn't kept his fangs. "Oh no, you'll be wearing that ring for the next seven days."

Seht choked. "*Seven* days . . . I'll go mad!"

Ravnos turned and stepped toward the door. "As you pointed out . . ." He opened the door and turned to smile at Seht. "I *am* a sadist." He waved Seht toward the door. "Shall we go to the meeting?"

Seht stepped toward the door and passed Ravnos scowling ferociously, showing his fangs. "You're damned lucky you caught me. If I'd caught you . . ."

"Are you *sure* you want to give me ideas?" Ravnos hit the button to close and lock the door behind him.

Seht looked away and folded his arms across his chest. "Calling you a sadist was an understatement."

Ravnos lunged forward to pin Seht to the wall behind him

by his shoulders.

Seht's eyes opened wide, and his lips parted, pink and damp, and oh so tempting.

Ravnos pressed his mouth to Seht's and slid his tongue past those sharp fangs to taste him. Wet, hot, and a hint of that feral musk he could never get out of his dreams . . .

Seht grabbed onto Ravnos's shoulders and returned the kiss with interest, chasing Ravnos's tongue with nipping teeth.

It took more effort than he cared to admit for Ravnos to release Seht's lips. He pressed his brow to Seht's. "You don't have to put up with this. You can leave at any time."

Seht licked his lips and stared straight into Ravnos's eyes. "Do your worst. I will not leave you."

Ravnos nodded and stepped back to straighten his cravat. "We will see."

Seht smiled, showing his long teeth. "Yes, we will."

APPENDIX

The Language of the Skeldhi

Skeldhor Prime — Seht's home world

Skeldhi — the people of Skeldhor Prime, Imperium ship-speak bastardization of *skeldyht* / . . . of Skeldhor

-dhyt — (pl.) the people of . . .

Kwusehyr — a principal spaceport

rahyt — blood-rage

Tawrhyt — skeldhi ovulation cycle / implies 'season of sacred blood'

Titles

- *mehnat* — royal (ornamental) collar

'Sey — lady mistress (pronounced: say)

'Syr — lord master (pronounced: seer)

'Syr'dhyt — generic lord master / . . . of an office

A'sey — respectable ma'am (non-royal)

A'syr — respectable sir (non-royal)

Atehf-mehnat — Queen's Consort / implies 'collared prince'

Atehf — prince consort

Deshryt — blood prince; direct relation to royal line / . . . of the blood

Dhe'syah — moon blade (weapon), also sworn vassal or liege man / implies "the lord's weapon"

Hedjhyt — crown princess

Kehpresh — war prince

Mehnat — royal (ornamental) collar

Pshent — Queen / implies 'Mother'

Sey'dhyt—generic lady mistress / . . . of an office
Syrdhyt—generic lord master / . . . of an office
Tahemryt—blood princess; direct relation to royal line / . . . of the blood

Law & Government

Maht—Law—Honor—Truth; the world order, justice, proper conduct

Ehnyad—The Council of Nine Elders
- *Ehnya'dhyt*—councilor / . . . of the council

Mahfeht—office of judicial enforcement and legal execution
- *Mahfeht'syr*—lord master executioner
- *Mahf'dhyt*—enforcer, also known as a hunter / . . . of judicial authority; legal executioner

Mehdjay—office of Intelligence and Security
- *Mehdjay'syr*—Lord-officer of Intelligence and Security
- *mehdja'dhyt*—Investigative Officer

Sehnbay—office of medicine / implies health
- *Sehnbay'syr*—master surgeon-engineer
- *sehn'dhyt*—medic / . . . of health

Uhra'eh—Office of the Military / implies "a group of fire-spitting serpents"
- *Uhra'eh'syr*—warlord / implies "Lord of the fire-spitting serpents"
- *uhra'dhyt*—a soldier / . . . of the fire-spitting serpents

Pets

deyjaht—skilled or trained rehkyt (m.) / implies 'educated male'
- *Nehkyx*—a punisher or trainer / implies 'whip'
- *Nehkyx'a'syr*—principal trainer

isfeht — outlaw; runaway rehkyt / implies disorderly, chaotic, insane

rekhyt — pet / implies 'captive bird'

seysaht — skilled or trained rehkyt (f.) / implies 'educated female'

seysehn — concubine / implies 'lotus flower'

shen — rehkyt obedience collar / implies 'to encircle'

teht — rehkyt in ovulation cycle / implies 'sacred blood'

upuaht — rehkyt guard / implies 'canine guardian'

ABOUT THE AUTHOR

Morgan Hawke

"For me, writing is more than a passion it's an *obsession*. The stories crowd into my head. I write them down so I can get some peace. Where do I get my ideas? Rampant curiosity. I play the game of 'What If?' with everything I encounter. Everything I do and everything I see triggers a story to be told. I am a voracious reader of Romance, Science-Fiction, Fantasy, Horror and Erotica, so naturally my stories follow along the lines of what I like to read."

Morgan Hawke has lived in seven states of the US and spent two years in England. She has been an auto mechanic, a security guard, a waitress, a groom in a horse-stable, in the military, a copywriter, a magazine editor, a professional tarot reader, a belly-dancer and a stripper. Her personal area of expertise is the strange and unusual.

Ms. Hawke has been writing erotic fiction since 1998 and maintains a close and personal relationship with her computer and her cat.